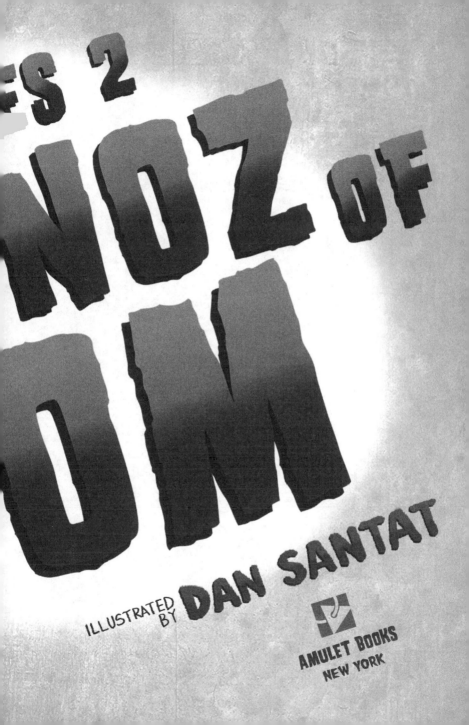

ES 2

NOZ OF

OM

ILLUSTRATED BY **DAN SANTAT**

AMULET BOOKS
NEW YORK

PUBLISHER'S NOTE: This is a work of fiction. Names. characters. places. and incidents are either the product of the author's imagination or used fictitiously. and any resemblance to actual persons. living or dead. business establishments. events. or locales is entirely coincidental.

Library of Congress Cataloging-in-Publication Data

Beaty. Andrea.
The Schnoz of Doom / Andrea Beaty ; illustrated by Dan Santat.
pages cm. — (Fluffy bunnies ; 2)
ISBN 978-1-4197-1051-3 (hardcover) — ISBN 978-1-61312-759-9 (ebook)
[1. Extraterrestrial beings—Fiction. 2. Smell—Fiction. 3. Twins—Fiction. 4. Brothers and sisters—Fiction. 5. Humorous stories.] I. Santat. Dan, illustrator. II. Title.
PZ7.B380547Sc 2015
[Fic]—dc23
2014038769

Printed and bound in U.S.A.
10 9 8 7 6 5 4 3 2 1

Amulet Books are available at special discounts when purchased in quantity for premiums and promotions as well as fundraising or educational use. Special editions can also be created to specification. For details. contact specialsales@abramsbooks.com or the address below.

ABRAMS
THE ART OF BOOKS SINCE 1949

115 West 18th Street
New York. NY 10011
www.abramsbooks.com

For John

ACKNOWLEDGMENTS

Some people think that Fierce, Obnoxious, Odoriferous
Furballs are fictional creatures. That is too bad for them,
because it means that they will not be prepared in case of
an actual Foof attack. I do not have that problem. I have
bunions. In case you do not know what bunions are, I will
tell you. Bunions are what you get when you cross bunnies
with onions. That is a lie, but it does not matter. What
matters is that I have many people who know all about
Foofs and who will help me ~~if~~ when they attack.

Thank you, thank you, thank you, Erica Finkel, Susan Van
Metre, Dan Santat, Pam Notarantonio, Chad Beckerman,
Jen Graham, Nicole Russo, and Jason Wells.

Thanks to Edward Necarsulmer IV, Andrew and Katie, the
Urams, and (of course) the Beatys. Special thanks to Michael
Uram, who invented the Birds and Others Classification
System of Things in the Universe, which will be very useful
indeed when the Foofs attack. Hint: They are Others.

Chapter 1

When suddenly . . .

A massive bubble of gas erupted from the murky bottom of Putrescent Pond and oozed upward through the stinking pool of thick gray slime. The bubble pushed against the pond's oily skin, which bulged into an enormous greasy dome.

Three ragged gray creatures with swirly blue eyes stood on the shore and watched intently. They tilted their heads to one side, pointed their enormous schnozzles toward the dome, stamped their puny feet impatiently, and sniffed hungrily.

Remember this. It's important later.

Chapter 2

Perhaps that illustration makes you uneasy. Perhaps it rings a bell* or stirs a vague memory of another race of fierce creatures you once read about: the Fluffs (Fierce, Large, Ugly, and Ferocious Furballs). If so, we are sorry to bring back such dreadful memories, but the truth is that these bunnies remind you of Fluffs because they are related. They originated on the planet of the Fluffs. They looked like Fluffs. They acted like Fluffs. In fact, they *were* Fluffs. The worst kind of Fluffs. Fluffs from a clan so horrific . . . so hideous . . . so heinous . . . so horrible that the *Merriam-Webster Dictionary* ran out of H-words to describe them. In fact, the Clan was so evil that, during the Great Pudding Wars, the other Fluffs sent them hurling into space using an intergalactic slingshot. The Clan landed on a nauseating planet covered with stinking, swampy, oozing slime pits and stench ponds. They called it Stenchopia.

*"Rings a bell" is simply an expression. If you hear actual bells at this moment, you should either (a) get your hearing checked or (b) stop reading books at train crossings. Seriously. Go to a library. It's more comfortable AND it's safer.

You might ask yourself what this clan of Fluffs did that was so horrible that it made their own cousins slingshot them into space. However, asking yourself is not useful. If you do *not* already know the answer, how could you reply? And if you *do* already know the answer, why ask in the first place? It makes more sense for you to ask us, since we brought it up. Let's start over.

So, you ask, "What could be so offensive to Fluffs that they would exile their own cousins to the armpit of the universe without a can of deodorant to protect them?"

Good question. Against our better judgment, we will tell you. However, to prevent your brain from exploding from such unsettling information, we will allow the publisher to review our comments and remove any dangerous bits.

Here is the answer:

They ██████████████████████████ on the ██████ ████████████████████, which was a bit like putting ██████ on ████████████████ with peanut butter. Then, ██████ ████████ fluffy kittens ████████ and slightly ████████████ but never chewy. Until ████████████████, which nobody saw coming! It singed their ████████████████████████████, resulting in ████████████████████████████ and most of all: ████████████████████████████. Sure, they all had a big laugh about it later, but at the time, it was enough to make the Fluffs ████████████████, which you can't put into a basket no matter how hard you try.

Well, now that you know, it's time to move on.

Chapter 3

Warning: You might want to hold your nose for this next part. Also, if you're eating while you read, you might consider finishing that before you continue this, unless you are reading during your school lunch. If so, good for you. Reading is an important part of every meal. (This message paid for by a bribe from your English teacher.)

The conditions on Stenchopia were difficult, and many Fluffs could not survive. The rest adapted through the generations, and the Clan changed.

Back on their home planet, Fluffs absorbed the energy of the sugary atmosphere through the clear hollow tubules of their fur. These tubules also acted as tiny telepathic transmitters that sent their brain waves to those around them. When coupled with their hypnotic swirly eyes, the Fluffs could control the minds of anyone. Once they devoured a creature, they could transmit the entire form of that creature to the mind of anyone they hypnotized. It was a camouflage that made them lethal.

However, on Stenchopia, the hollow tubules of the

Fluffs' fur quickly gummed up with swamp slime, so they could not transmit telepathic signals. Even worse, without a sugary atmosphere (which was lacking on Stenchopia), the Fluffs had no food source. They shrank. Many perished. But not all.

Those Fluffs with bigger noses than the others sniffed in the stinky air of Stenchopia and found traces of energy in the putrid vapors wafting off the stench ponds. It was not much energy, but it was enough to survive. Those survivors passed the genes for their larger noses on to the next generation, who passed them on to the next generation, who . . . blah blah next generation blah blah next blah blah . . . you get the idea. Ultimately, those with the biggest, most efficient noses survived and thrived. Through the generations, their noses became magnificent wobbling schnozzles that could efficiently harvest the power of stench. This was the power of the schnoz.

Other traits also developed through the generations. The Clan's feet shrank. Their once clear, hollow fur became dull and gray and coarse. While descendants of the original Clan no longer communicated telepathically using their hollow-tubed fur, they developed an amazing new power of communication: They talked.

Actually, that was not very amazing. You probably do it all the time. But you probably can't control anybody's mind with your brain. The Clan could. The pathways connecting their brains and their schnozzles developed into a sophisticated network capable of transmitting telepathic signals via smell. Smellepathy.

Smellepathic signals sent images, feelings, and ideas to the brains of others, leaving them at the mercy of the large-schnozzled Clan. When added to their hypnotic swirly-eyed gaze, this power made the Clan unstoppable. Like their cousins, they used the identity of devoured creatures as camouflage and tricked the planet's animals into doing things for them, like becoming snacks. Although the Clan gathered energy through their enormous schnozzles, they still loved a good snack, in the same way that people enjoy popcorn. It has no nutritional value, but oh, that crunch!

And so it was that over many generations, the Clan became a completely new race of fluffy bunnies. Very, very stinky bunnies.

They became the Fierce, Obnoxious, Odoriferous Furballs.

Foofs.

And the rest—as they say—is history.

Table 1: Know Your Foof, taken from *The Illustrated Guide to Fluffs and Other Space Creatures You Don't Want to Meet*, by Professor Donald J. Dewdy. (Work unpublished.) Perhaps you remember a similar chart in *Attack of the Fluffy Bunnies*. In that chart, Professor Donald J. Dewdy offered a comparison between the Fierce, Large, Ugly, and Ferocious Furballs (Fluffs) and simple Earth rabbits or, as you might call them, bunnies. In the following table, Professor Dewdy offers a comparative analysis between the Fierce, Obnoxious, Odoriferous Furballs (Foofs) and chocolate. No one knows why Professor Dewdy chose to compare aliens with a delicious treat instead of something useful like a human or another alien, but we are sure that he had a good reason. Or maybe he was just hungry. In the end, it doesn't matter. What does matter is that if you wish to have a delicious warm drink, melt chocolate into a glass of hot milk, stir, and add whipped cream. Do not melt a Foof in a glass of hot milk, stir, or add whipped cream. It wastes the whipped cream and annoys the Foof.

TABLE 1: KNOW YOUR FOOF

	CHOCOLATE	FOOFS
Genus and species	Chocolate is not a living thing and does not have a genus or species. It is, however, made from the seeds of the cacao tree or cocoa tree. Actually, they are the same tree, but one name is for people who like the letter "a" while the other is for people who prefer the letter "o." People who love the letter "v" are weirdos who probably don't like chocolate at all.	*Lepus foofilicious*
Habitat	On top of cakes. In flat bars wrapped in thin silver foil. Swimming in cups of hot milk with floating islands of whipped cream. Yum.	The putrescent slime ponds of Stenchopia in the Stinkpit System
Diet	Chocolate and diets are like matter and antimatter. They cancel each other out in a gigantic explosion, after which nothing matters.	Foofs ingest "nutrients" by inhaling the gaseous bubbles that burst forth from the putrid ponds on their planets. When they receive enough nutrition, the Foofs' extreme metabolism gives them ridiculous strength and lets them grow to enormous heights of 7 feet or more.

	CHOCOLATE	FOOFS
Communication	It is a basic law of the universe that inanimate objects cannot communicate with living beings. Because of this law (also known as the Hershey's Principle), chocolate cannot communicate with people. It does not have—wow . . . is that a bonbon?—the ability to in any way influence—must have bonbon—thought patterns and . . . yummmmmmm. Correction: Chocolate possesses the most powerful property for communication in the universe. It is delicious.	Smellepathy: Foofs control the brains of other creatures via smell. Smellepathic signals send images, feelings, and ideas to the brains of creatures under their control. Under rare and very, very, VERY smelly conditions, the Foofs' brains heat to a level that fuses the neural-telepathic pathways, making the creatures permanently under the Foofs' control. Smellepathy controls their prey's brain via the olfactory nerves. The word "olfactory," which means smelling, should not be confused with "old factory," because that would be silly. To enhance this process, the Foofs emit a "fragrance" that is sometimes confused with the sweet smell of roses outside a perfume factory on a perfect summer morning after a lovely rain shower. Ha ha ha ha ha. That's a good one.
Predators	Everyone who ever lived. And their grandmothers. Really. How could you not know that?	Yes, they are.

Chapter 4

Remember that slime-covered stench bubble at Putrescent Pond? Here's an update:

Chapter 5

When suddenly . . .

Joules Rockman lay in her bed with the covers over her head. That was a lie. There was nothing sudden about this. It was, however, a catchy way to start a new chapter. We hope you enjoyed it.

Joules Rockman did not enjoy it. Like most people who like oxygen, she did *not* enjoy covers over her head. What Joules *did* enjoy was breathing, a task that was especially difficult when her mother cooked breakfast, which, sadly, was every day. Most people consider it a comforting treat for their mother to cook them breakfast. However, most people's mothers were not Mrs. Rockman.

Both of Joules's parents, Mr. and Mrs. Rockman, were lovely people, but they were not gourmet cooks. They were scientists and "extreme experimental" cooks. As scientists, they were more interested in the chemical reactions of cooking than in flavor. Sometimes, their resulting dishes were astonishing. And occasionally, astonishingly delicious.

Most, however, were not. Still, every meal with the Rockmans was a thrill. Just not in a good way.

While Joules and her twin, Kevin, were less than enthusiastic about their parents' cooking, they knew it was one small way in which their parents showed their love. That was very sweet. Even if it was not sweet smelling. Not wanting to hurt their parents' feelings, Joules and Kevin nodded politely and said "yum" when asked about their parents' cooking creations. They also became experts at ditching their meals without being seen and fending for themselves. In fact, they became very good (and rather sneaky) cooks.

Still, waking up to an unknown vapor that smelled up the house made Joules cranky. She got dressed and dragged herself to the kitchen, where Kevin sat behind a steaming bowl of unidentifiable chunky purplish soup. Kevin held a spoon in one hand and a pen in the other. He jotted something in his notebook, observed the fumes rising from the bowl, crossed out his note, and wrote something new. Halfway through his scribbling, he paused and—

ahhh-choo!

Kevin sprayed a fine mist over his bowl and half the table. Joules rolled her eyes.

"Nice," she said while Kevin wiped his nose with a napkin. "The idea is to sneeze *into* the napkin instead of blowing snot all over the table."

"Sorry," Kevin said and went back to scribbling in his notebook.

Most people would be horrified by a germ shower in their breakfast, but Kevin didn't worry about it. It wasn't breakfast, because there was no way he was going to eat it. Kevin was studying it. Plus, his nose was too stuffed up to smell the nasty fumes that wafted up from the bowl. Usually, being stuffed up is not a good thing. When sitting in front of a steaming bowl of purple breakfast soup, it is a very good thing indeed.

Mrs. Rockman entered the kitchen and gave Joules a quick hug.

"Good morning, darling," she said.

Mrs. Rockman pulled open the refrigerator door.

"Cheese spray!" she said. "That's what your curried-kale-SPAMberry breakfast soup needs! What could be better?"

Joules could think of two million and seven things that would be better (none of them involving breakfast soup), but she simply shrugged.

Mrs. Rockman stuck her head and half of her torso into the fridge and tossed jars of unrecognizable liquids onto the floor behind her.

"It's in here somewhere," she said.

Kevin and Joules shot a glance at each other and made their move. Joules grabbed two paper bag lunches and a box of Pop-Tarts she had stashed under the living room couch the night before and ran out the front door. Kevin swept up his notebook, grabbed two backpacks from the hallway, and ran out the back door. They met at the driveway. Kevin dropped the backpacks on the asphalt as Joules handed him a bag and a pouch of Pop-Tarts.

"Thanks," said Kevin.

"No problem," said Joules. "That was a super-fumilicious breakfast."

"I'm pretty sure that's not a word," said Kevin.

"I'm pretty sure that wasn't breakfast."

Kevin nodded, ripped open the foil packet, and devoured a Pop-Tart. Then he stuffed his notebook and lunch bag into his backpack.

Just then, a white van sped by. The driver flung a rolled-up newspaper out the window. It skidded over the asphalt and flopped open at Kevin's feet. The left half of the paper was filled with a photo of a crashed rocket in a forest clearing.

Joules and Kevin Rockman looked at the paper. They looked at each other. They looked at the paper again. The headline read: "Rocket Crashes Near Old Snottie's Tissue Factory."

They scanned the article. Except for the advertisements plastered all over the rocket, it was almost identical to one they had seen at Camp Whatsitooya, where they went to summer camp. That rocket had transported three deadly alien rabbits to Earth. Alien rabbits that had nearly taken over Earth, we might add.

What might this one have transported?

"This is bad," said Joules. "Really bad."

"I know," said Kevin. "Listen to this! The mayor says that 'the rocket is absolutely safe and there's nothing that could possibly be dangerous about it. There is no need to worry. Really! What could possibly go wrong?'"

Joules sighed and shook her head.

"Famous Last Words," she said.

"Yep," said Kevin.

"You know what that means," said Joules.

"Yep," said Kevin.

"I hate Famous Last Words," said Joules.

"Yep," said Kevin.

Joules and Kevin Rockman adjusted their backpacks and trekked down the boring sidewalk of their boring town toward their boring school. As they went, they had an uneasy feeling that none of these things would remain boring for long.

The History of TBD School

People say that TBD School was named after Dr. Tom B. Deter. That is not true. Dr. Tom B. Deter is an imaginary doctor made up by the school secretary responsible for ordering the school's sign. She used the common placeholder—TBD, which means To Be Determined—on the order form. When the board met to decide the actual school name, it was her job to change the form and mail it in. Alas, the board meeting was the same night as the finale of her favorite television show: *America Lacks Talent.*

Instead of going to the meeting, she mailed in the form and stayed home. To be fair, the finale was a real nail-biter between a real nail-biter (Chewie Larue) who chewed his fingernails *and* his toenails and a lady who could grow her nose hairs really fast. (Spoiler: Chewie Larue won.)

Three days later, the sign arrived and was

hoisted onto the school roof. It announced to the world that the school was named TBD School. Instead of sending it back, which would take minutes of effort, the secretary made up a story to explain the name. She invented Dr. Tom B. Deter (Dr. TBD), the famous scientist who had cured Stiff Upper Lipitosis. The board members did not protest, because they had also stayed home to watch *America Lacks Talent* and missed the school-naming meeting.

The town citizens did not protest, either. They believed that since nobody in town had Stiff Upper Lipitosis, someone must have cured it. Nobody wanted to look stupid by saying, "Hey, that sounds like a bogus disease. Are you sure that happened?" Instead, they all looked stupid by pretending it was true. Everyone was happy.

The town embraced the new school identity and named the school basketball team the Fighting Question Marks.

School chant: "Go? Go? Go?"

Chapter 6

When the twins reached the front door of TBD School, they were greeted by Principal Posner. Principal Posner was a plump woman who rarely smiled. She believed that smiling took too much time, and she was far too efficient for that. When the Rockman twins arrived, she stood in the entryway beside a kid wrapped from head to ankle in Ace bandages. Only the kid's red high-top sneakers showed.

"Hey, Andrew," said Joules to the mummified student.

"Mmmmmm," the kid mumbled through the Ace bandages.

"That's not Andrew," said Kevin. "It's Katie. Or maybe Derek."

"Whatever," said Joules.

"You're late!" said Principal Posner.

Kevin looked at his watch. There were five minutes left until the bell rang.

"I'm early," he said.

"Hmmmm," said the principal, narrowing her eyes suspiciously at him.

Being on time was a form of tardiness to Principal Posner. She was a precise person. She could tell the time to the exact second without looking at a clock. Timekeeping wasn't the only thing Principal Posner took to the extreme. She was a former member of the U.S. Army Ambulance Corps and current national champion on the Tourniquet Drill Team. She took any and every opportunity to stay in tip-top bandaging form. Thus, any kid slow enough to catch her eye became an unwilling practice "patient" and ended up looking like King Tut. Principal Posner reached into the satchel she carried with her at all times and pulled out a thick roll of cotton bandages.

"Where is my splint?" she said, digging through the satchel.

Joules and Kevin did not stick around to find out. They sprinted down the hall to their first class, biology. It was the first class of the day that they would have together. It would not be the last. Unlike some schools that put twins in separate classes so each student could have a "unique educational experience," TBD School had put the Rockman twins in all the same classes since their very first day of kindergarten.

This was not a function of educational philosophy but bad eyesight on the part of the school secretary who'd registered the twins for kindergarten. She'd looked at the two registration forms and thought she was seeing double. Instead of finding her glasses, which were atop her head, she simply enrolled one student: Kevin Joules Rockman. Being enrolled as a single student had very few drawbacks, but it had two big advantages: half the amount of homework and twice the brainpower on tests. Kevin excelled in some subjects and Joules in others. Between them, they made one exceptional student.

The twins had their own strengths and talents. Kevin was organized and methodical. He took great notes and kept charts of anything that might be important: due dates for assignments, vocabulary words, and information about the teachers' children and pets. This last item was very useful for distracting teachers from giving pop quizzes. For instance, a timely question about Fido's struggle with fleas could disrupt any pop quiz in English class. (Note: Fido McMallow is the English teacher's son and should not be confused with her dog, Billy.)

Where Kevin was methodical, Joules was spontaneous. Rather than face a situation with facts and figures as Kevin might, Joules liked to poke new situations with a stick. For many students like Joules, school presents challenges, but

Joules learned early on that while sticks from trees were forbidden in school, small pointy sticks with graphite tips were encouraged. Armed with a fine set of No. 2 pencils, Joules thrived.

Upon arriving in Mr. H's biology class, the twins settled into seats next to each other at a long lab table. They looked around to see what was new in the classroom. There was always something new to see in biology class. Mr. H was a collector of all things scientific. And since everything that exists involves science, the room was stuffed. In fact, the shelves were stuffed with stuffed stuff like taxidermied chipmunks, snakes, sloths, and other animals. The counters were piled with petri dishes and jars of odd-colored liquids.

Joules and Kevin liked biology class. Partly because of all the weird things to look at, but mostly, they liked Mr. H. He was a quirky man. Clueless even. But his cluelessness came from being too busy to notice un-important things like matching socks or shoes or correctly buttoned shirts. Mr. H was too busy for those things because he was so busy being passionate about science. Other kids made fun of Mr. H behind his back, and sometimes to his face, even though it skipped right past him. Joules and Kevin never did that. In truth, they felt a little protective of Mr. H. They didn't have to think further back than breakfast to know that sometimes passionate but clueless people have the biggest hearts.

A Field Guide to Scientists

Not all scientists look like Mr. H. That is a good thing. If they did, it would be very confusing for his children. How can you tell if a person is a scientist? If they are doing science, they are a scientist. Phew. That was incredibly easy.

Chapter 7

It took only a second for Kevin and Joules to find the day's new object in the cluttered biology classroom. It was a dog crate on the floor by Mr. H's desk. The cage was intended for a medium-sized dog. Perhaps a Labrador or a poodle, or a Labradoodle or a cocka-doodle-do-poo.

However, there was not a dog in the dog cage. There was, instead, a rabbit. A small gray rabbit the color of swamp slime. It did not look like any rabbit the twins had seen in their yards. However, there was something familiar about it. It was something about the swirly eyes. The twins wanted to investigate, but before they could get up, Mr. H entered the room and tossed his tweed hat onto the table. He hung his tweed jacket on a coatrack. Correction: Mr. H did not hang his jacket on a coatrack. He hung his jacket on Mack Buckley, who was sitting at his lab table with his hand raised. Mack was an eager student and was always the first to answer questions. Often before they were asked. His hand was perpetually raised, leading Mr. H to confuse him with a coatrack.

It was an easy mistake for anyone. It was a daily mistake for Mr. H, who was a keen observer of science and completely blind to everything else. It is important to note that besides being passionate, he was also brilliant. In fact, Mr. H was an actual college professor. He was the head of biological studies at South-Northwestern University. One day, while driving to campus, he was distracted by a migration of Canada geese and ended up at TBD School. He went into the biology classroom, where he found a group of ridiculously short college freshmen. Assuming that their shortness was due to a vitamin deficiency (and not to the fact that they were fifth graders), he suggested they eat taller vegetables and got on with the day's lesson. He had been teaching at TBD School ever since.

Mr. H sat down at his desk, pushed his round glasses up the bridge of his nose, and shuffled through a mountain of papers. After twenty-five minutes, he looked up and noticed twenty-six short college freshmen staring at him.

"AAAAHHHGH!" he screamed. "Who are you?"

"Your class," said the class.

"What are you doing here?"

"Having class?"

"What am I doing here?"

"Teaching class?"

Mr. H thought about it for a moment, flipped through his appointment book, and then slammed it shut.

"You're late!" he said. "We should have started twenty-five minutes ago."

Tom Barton snickered. Joules gave Tom the stink-eye. He quit snickering. It was a typical day.

Here is a handy-dandy chart for those of you who have been too busy doing useful things to keep up with the ever-growing list of dog breeds.		
Labrador	Poodle	Labradoodle
Labrador retriever	La-Z-Boy recliner	Labrador get-it-yourself-er
Scooby-Doo	Poodle	Scooby-doodle
Poodle	Snickers bar	Snicker-doodle
Cocker spaniel	Poodle	Cockapoo
Cocker spaniel	Rooster	Cocka-doodle-do
Cockapoo	Rooster	Cocka-doodle-do-poo
Cockapoo	Boxer	Box-a-poo
Chihuahua	Saint Bernard	Chihuanard
Great Dane	Awful Dane	So-so Dane
Pomeranian	A very hard rock	Pome-granite—get it? Huh? Huh? Like the fruit? Pomegranate.

Chapter 8

Mr. H began his lecture. The topic of the day was taxonomy, which is the study of taxes. Ha! No, it's not! Made you look.

Actually, taxonomy is the study of grouping things. Classification systems, if you want to get fancy. Mr. H did not want to get fancy. He liked things simple and had developed his own system of classifying things in the universe. He called it the Birds and Others Classification System of Things in the Universe. In his system, things are identified by the answer to one simple question: Can it fly? If the answer is yes, it is a bird. If the answer is no, it is an Other. Those of you interested in learning more should refer to the chart in Kevin's notes. Those of you not interested in learning more should remember that education is an important part of every meal. (This message paid for by another bribe from your English teacher.)

BIRDS AND OTHERS CLASSIFICATION SYSTEM OF THINGS IN THE UNIVERSE

BIRDS	OTHERS
Canaries, parakeets, hawks, eagles, and other feathered creatures that fly	Penguins—Honestly. Who are they kidding with those feathers?
Butterflies	Ostriches—Except ostriches on airplanes
Moths	
Helicopters	People—Except when riding ostriches on airplanes
Airplanes	
Paper airplanes	Fish—Except flying fish
Paper wads	Cars—Except flying cars, which really should be invented by now
Baseballs	
Footballs	Rocks, scissors, and paper
Soccer balls during a goal kick	Skiers who don't jump
Flying squirrels	Skiers not on ski lifts. Anything flying through the air on a ski lift is a bird.
Flying fish	
Flying Wallendas	
Gymnasts	Trees
Kites	Books—Except the kind they talk about in movies when they say, "Throw the book at 'em." While the books are actually being thrown, they are flying, and therefore they are birds.
Ski jumpers	
Snowballs	
Leaves in October	

A Note About Taxonomy

(Warning: If you find this boring, do not panic. Some people do. Others do not. And by Others, we mean *not* birds. See the chart on page 35.)

Scientists use taxonomy to group and name organisms. It helps scientists understand how living things are similar and how they are different. It also helps them remember which drawer in the lab contains live snakes and which one contains mice. That's good to know before you reach inside a drawer.

You might be familiar with a system of taxonomy created by the famous eighteenth-century Swedish botanist named Carolus Linnaeus. Carolus was famous for having a girlish name (and figure). He was also famous for organizing and naming living things based on the origins of their physical structures. It is the system used by most scientists in the world. He used two Latin names to describe each organism. He called it binomial nomenclature, which—any way you cut it—was a better name than Carolus Linnaeus.

Other famous systems of taxonomy classify organisms by color, ability to dance, or how they look in a dress. Note: All scientists agree that, despite their knobby knees, giraffes look much better in dresses than tree sloths, which have no fashion sense at all.

Mr. H ended his lecture with a challenge.

"I will give extra credit to anyone bringing in specimens of Birds and Others," he said.

A muffled "Woo-hoo" escaped from beneath Mr. H's jacket. Mr. H had just made Mack's day. Mack was a professional extra-credit collector and had earned 257,143 extra-credit points since kindergarten. Mack had enough extra credit to ensure As in all his classes through graduate school—for his whole family. If extra-credit points could buy things, Mack would have a personal jet.

Joules, on the other hand, did not care about extra credit. With a little bit of work (from Kevin), they would probably get an A in the class, or at least a B or maybe a C. After all, what was the point of doing extra credit when you could spend your time doing something useful like *not* doing extra credit?

Your English teacher would like to insert an emergency announcement here suggesting that you follow Mack's example and not that of Joules in regard to extra credit. After all, extra credit is an important part of every meal.

We would also like to warn you not to take Joules's lack of interest in extra credit as a lack of intelligence. Doing so would be unwise. Just ask Mack Buckley about that. Mack had been completely obliterated (which means being stomped flat) by Joules at last year's Math & Science Quiz-O-Rama and Sushi Festival. Joules didn't care about extra credit, but she was smart and she liked a competition.

In either case, Joules had spent the class digging a hole in her biology book with her sharp stick (a.k.a. pencil). But Mr. H's next words made her drop her pencil and pay attention. Mr. H walked to the cage on the floor and lifted it up for everyone to see.

"I must show you a very unusual specimen I discovered near the old Snottie's Tissue Factory!" said Mr. H. "I have never seen another Other like this Other, and I wish to study it further. I will give an automatic A in this class and a piece of cake to anyone who brings in another Other like it!"

Normally, the word "cake" would have gotten Joules's attention immediately. Saying that Joules loved cake is like saying that cats love video cameras. The abundance of adorable videos on the Internet proves that is true. If cats did not love video cameras, why would they make so many funny movies?

This time, however, the mention of cake barely registered with her. The words that got her attention were "old Snottie's Tissue Factory." She looked at Kevin, who looked back at her with a worried expression.

What were the odds that Mr. H would send his students on a quest to find a weird swirly-eyed rabbit near an abandoned tissue factory on the very same day that the newspaper reported a crashed rocket near the same factory?

We can tell you the odds. They were very, very odd indeed! Nobody knew that better than the Rockman twins. They had seen enough science fiction thrillers on *The Late, Late, Late Creepy Show for Insomniacs* to know that coincidences did not happen. Ever. Anyone who thought otherwise was destined to die a terrible, horrible sci-fi-movie death. As terrible, horrible deaths go, those are the most terrible and most horrible. If you doubt that, just ask the guy from *Koalas of Death*. Oh wait, you can't! He's dead!

Kevin leaned closer to Joules.

"We need to get a better look at that rabbit," he whispered.

"Let's—" Joules began, but the bell rang and her whisper was drowned out by the clamor of students grabbing their books and hustling out of the room.

The twins jumped from their seats, but before they reached Mr. H, he swung the dog crate onto the counter. The rabbit drummed its feet furiously and stared out the cage with a crazed swirly-eyed look.

"Mr. H," said Kevin, "can we look at that rabbit?"

"Ah! My favorite scientists!" said Mr. H. "How are you Rockmans today?"

"We're fine, Mr. H," said Joules. "But we'd like to get a closer look at that rabbit."

"It's an Other," said Mr. H. "Those noisy short freshmen have made it very nervous, and it needs silence." He raised his finger to his lips. "Shhhhhh!"

He gently shushed the twins and plucked his jacket off Mack, who swept up his books and scurried out of class in search of more extra credit. Mr. H draped the jacket over the cage.

"You can see it tomorrow," he said. "It's a beautiful specimen."

"It might be dangerous!" said Kevin.

"That's where you are wrong, Kevin," said Mr. H. "Birds are dangerous! Especially those big ones with propellers. A little Other like this couldn't hurt anyone."

"But . . . ," said Joules.

"I admire your keen interest," said Mr. H. "It makes me hopeful for the future of science. But there's no danger here. This is just a fluffy little Other with a rather large nose and swirly, swirly—"

A glazed look passed over his face.

"They are fascinating eyes," said Mr. H. "Very interesting eyes . . ."

He paused.

"Mr. H?" said Kevin.

"Hello, Kevin!" said Mr. H, looking at Kevin as if for the first time. "Shouldn't you get to class? I'm going to leave this Other right here in this cage in a building with hundreds of schoolchildren nearby. What could possibly go wrong?"

They wanted to tell Mr. H that millions of things could go wrong, but he had turned away and was rifling through a smelly basket of mismatched gym socks he had collected from the gymnasium for a microbiology experiment.

Neither Joules nor Kevin spoke, but the same thought ran through both their minds as they grabbed their books and headed toward social studies class:

Famous Last Words.

Chapter 9

Remember that basket of adorable puppies from the last chapter? No? We don't, either. That is too bad. It would be pleasant to think about puppies right now. Instead, we must think about Foofs so that you understand what is going on. Those of you too frightened/spongy/your-adjective-here to think about Foofs should imagine puppies instead. This will not make you safer, but it might make you happier.

For an update on the Foofs, turn the page.

The Fierce, Obnoxious, Odoriferous Furballs took one last look at the wreckage of their beloved planet. They climbed into the rocket and pushed the giant button on the control panel marked "Push in case of butterfly toots."

With a deafening rumble, the engines ignited and the rocket shook violently. The Fierce, Obnoxious, Odoriferous Furballs did not notice. Their minds were filled with thoughts of bottled stench, enslaved humans, and soft, cottony tissues with a hint of lotion capable of soothing even the sorest schnoz.

The rocket jolted twice, then blasted into space toward a blue planet whose foolish creatures never suspected that they should run and hide while they still could.

Chapter 10

The remainder of the school day was boring for Joules and Kevin. Math was by the numbers and history was old news.

In the afternoon, though, a minor disaster occurred in Miss Chupakabra's third-grade classroom. During their annual Celebration of World Foods, a bowl of sauer-kraut collided with a jalapeño dip and a pot of stinky tofu. The new "food" released fumes that spread down the hall. Teachers slammed their classroom doors as the fumes overran their rooms. There were three exceptions: the lunchroom and the gym, which were filled with so many suspicious smells of their own that nobody noticed, and the biology room, where Mr. H was too busy to notice the fumes. He was classifying a fly that kept landing on his sandwich and then flying away. Each time it landed, the professor moved it from "Birds" to "Others" on his classification chart. It was time-consuming, and eraser-consuming as well.

Mr. H did not even notice when Miss Chupakabra brought him a large bowl of jala-sauer-fu to study. Like all the teachers at TBD School, she understood Mr. H's love of scientific investigation and often brought him curious things she found in her classroom. She left the bowl of fuming dip on the counter beside an unidentifiable and slightly hairy green glob that might have once been a kindergarten art project.

Besides Mr. H, the only other person at TBD School unaware of the putrid smell was Kevin. His nose was now completely stuffed, and he sneezed every few minutes. Joules was not so lucky and spent the afternoon holding her nose with one hand and writing with the other. Luckily, the last class of the day was physical education. Funky smells from the rest of the school had no power to match the aromas that dwelled in the gym.

Despite its aromas, Joules loved gym class. It was the one class of the day with real sticks: hockey sticks, lacrosse sticks, pole-vaulting sticks. Kevin was not so keen on gym. It was difficult doing pull-ups and push-ups with a notebook in his hand. However, he did not want to put his notebook down. It made him uneasy to be without it. Kevin's notes were a source of comfort to him, but more important, they were useful. His chart of Wiffle ball statistics told him exactly where to stand to avoid getting hit in the face by a Wiffle ball. Anyone who has ever experienced the painful red welts of Wiffle-face will understand.

For Kevin, the worst part of gym class was the teacher, Mr. Arnie Shwartzaninny. Or as everyone called him, Mr. Shhh. Not as an abbreviation of his long name, but because he had a voice that sounded like an airsick goose and nobody wanted to hear him talk.

As a boy, Mr. Shhh had suffered from a condition called noodle arms. Unable to do more than a few pull-ups, he was teased by gym-class bullies. This gave him great sympathy for noodle-armed kids. It also inspired him to invent a clever exercise contraption known as Noodle-Armor, which cured his noodle arms and made him a bazillionaire. Unlike other bazillionaires, who buy private islands and spend their lives keeping poor people off them, Mr. Shhh dedicated himself to helping the noodle-armed youth of America. He volunteered as the gym teacher at TBD School, where he helped fifth graders live better lives through upper-arm development.

Mr. Shhh had enormous, muscular arms sticking out of his V-shaped body, which dwindled from his very wide shoulders to his tiny pointy feet.

Because Kevin had difficulty with pull-ups, Mr. Shhh considered him a challenge and spent every class helping Kevin defeat his noodle arms. After ten minutes strapped into the Noodle-Armor, Kevin's arms didn't just look like noodles, they felt like noodles, too.

By the end of class, he was ready to go home. He was very sweaty and very stinky. And he was still stuffed up. While he couldn't smell anything, the way the other students fled when he came near was a pretty good clue that he needed to go home and shower. That was exactly what Kevin wanted to do.

Joules also wanted to get out of school. She wanted to get to the factory. Like Kevin, she worried that the arrival of these weird new rabbits spelled danger. Also, she wanted to beat Mack. Plus, there was a piece of cake at stake.

Even though they were in a hurry, they knew they had to check the biology room and see if Mr. H had the rabbit under control.

When the bell finally rang, Joules grabbed her backpack and Kevin's, since he was too tired to carry it himself. They headed back toward the biology room. On the way, they passed two second graders whose arms were bandaged together using the "human splint" maneuver. Well done,

Principal Posner! They also passed a mummy in red high-tops by the water fountain.

"Hey, Anna," said Joules.

"Mmmmmm!" said the mummy.

"That's Alexandra," said Kevin.

"Whatever," said Joules.

They stepped into the biology room. Mr. H was not there, but the dog cage was still on the counter. They stepped closer and looked at the weird gray rabbit. The rabbit glared at Kevin and Joules with swirling blue eyes and flashed its fangs.

"Do you remember the last time we saw a rabbit with eyes like that?" asked Joules.

"How could I forget?" asked Kevin. "This one is different, though. Look at that nose."

"Maybe it's just a rabbit."

Kevin leaned closer.

BAM! The rabbit slammed itself against the door of the cage. Kevin jumped back, knocking the bowl of jala-sauer-fu off the counter. The slimy green goo slopped over his pants.

"Ewww!" Kevin said, wiping it away with his hand. "Give me a paper towel."

He looked up, but Joules was already in the hallway.

"C'mon," she yelled. "We've got another rabbit to catch!"

"Thanks for the help!" Kevin said, shaking his hand and flinging a glob of goo through the air.

It landed on the rabbit, which sniffed hungrily and growled softly. Kevin picked up the empty bowl from the floor and put it back onto the counter beside the cage. He gave the rabbit one last look and ran after his sister.

The History of the Nose

The nose was invented by the ancient Tucanese people in 1400 BC as a display rack for eyeglasses. Since eyeglasses would not be invented for another 2,500 years, the nose failed miserably. (Note: Eyeglasses as we know them were invented in AD 1284 by an Italian named Salvino D'Armate, who also invented the phrase "You wouldn't hit a guy wearing these, would ya?")

During the late early period (AD 100–250) and the early late period (AD 100–250), the nose was used by nomadic ice herders as portable storage cabinets for nuts, berries, and other snacks. This practice was abandoned when the ice herders noticed local squirrels taking "a little too much interest" in their faces.

The nose increased in popularity after south Indian pepper farmers discovered the sneeze in AD 950. The nose gained further popularity when the Vikings began using it as a finger warmer on their long sea voyages. This ended with the Great Nostril Kerfuffle of AD 1000, when Fingnor the Lollygagger famously asked, "Vargr ok jörð heppni sefr?" and "Af járni er dómr?" which is Old Norse for "Whose finger is in my nostril?" and "Would it kill you to trim your nails?"

The most significant contribution of the nose came in California in 1849 when miner Frederick Snifflehanger discovered a green nugget in his nostril and reportedly said, "It's cold in here. I'm ill." His words were misheard by fellow miner and earwax collector Sherman

Hotzpilfer, who said, "There's gold in them thar hills?" His cry started a gold rush that lured 100,000 people to California. That might have turned out badly for Sherman. Luckily, there really *was* gold in them thar hills. Sherman Hotzpilfer became ridiculously rich and spent his entire fortune on earwax, which he carved into lifelike statues of famous people for tourists to admire.

Thank you, Nose.

Chapter 11

Remember the Fierce, Obnoxious, Odoriferous Furballs from earlier? Good! Otherwise, this would not make much sense to you! In any case, here is an update:

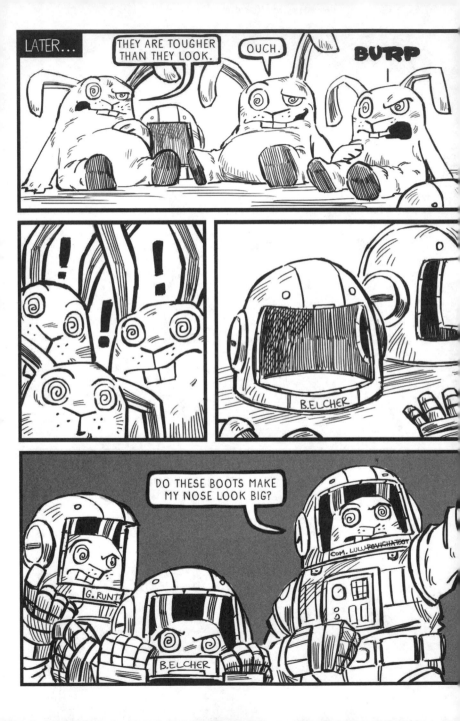

ARE YOU THINKING
WHAT I'M THINKING?

Chapter 12

Joules walked five steps in front of her brother on the way home. She was in a hurry to beat Mack to the factory. She was also trying to stay upwind from Kevin, who was a little on the smelly side. Okay, who are we kidding? Kevin reeked. Between his sweat from gym and the jala-sauer-fu on his pants, he was ripe. They reached the house and Joules unlocked the front door.

"Do I smell weird?" asked Kevin, trying to sniff the air through his stuffed-up nose.

"No," Joules lied. "You smell great. Wow! It's like you're wearing perfume."

"I should take a shower before—" Kevin started.

Joules gave him the stink-eye.

"—before I go to bed," Kevin continued.

"Good plan!" said Joules. "Let's roll."

Joules opened the door and the twins dumped the contents of their backpacks onto the living room couch. Joules pulled a new packet of Pop-Tarts from beneath the couch and tossed it into her backpack in case she got hungry later. Kevin packed his notebook and pen in case he got the urge to make a detailed list later.

The twins headed to the garage, where Joules grabbed her favorite (i.e., sharpened) hiking stick, and Kevin dug through a box of junk. The garage was filled with "ingredients" for Mr. and Mrs. Rockman's recipes. Among other things, there were dozens of different kinds of pickles, gallon jugs of taco sauce, enormous boxes of gelatin, and giant tubs of baking soda. Say what you will about extreme experimental cooking, it made hunting for things in the garage an adventure. Eventually, Kevin found what he was looking for behind a crate of dried prunes.

He held up his old butterfly net and frowned. It had seemed much bigger when he was three. Now it did not look big enough to hold a tiny moth, let alone a rabbit. Especially one with an enormous schnoz. Clearly, it was time to get a new net. He pulled out his notebook and made an entry in his List of Things I Need to Get Just in Case. If you are asking yourself, "In case of what?" the answer is yes.

Kevin and Joules hopped on their bikes and pedaled south past the edge of town. Joules biked upwind of Kevin, holding her hiking stick ahead of her like a jousting lance.

Kevin followed, holding the tiny butterfly net in front of his face to keep bugs away. Kevin was not a fan of bugs. Mostly because they were a big fan of him. Especially mosquitoes.

The old Snottie's Tissue Factory stood just beyond the edge of town near the Little Muddy River. The town founders had chosen the shores of the river, hoping to create a bustling manufacturing zone with transportation and power for factories. The first factory to arrive was Snottie's Tissue Factory. Unfortunately, it was also the last. The smells produced by the tissue factory kept its industrial neighbors at a distance (of 300 miles). The town gave up its dream of becoming an industrial power and also moved upwind. And so Snottie's Tissue Factory sat alone along the river, happily producing tissues to soothe the scratchy noses of people everywhere. When the economy faltered, the company bought a poor country in Eastern Europe, renamed it Snottiestan, and moved its factories overseas, leaving the redbrick factory on the shores of the Little Muddy River to decay. That was a decade ago. It had been vacant since then.

The twins biked to the boarded-up factory and leaned their bikes against the rough red brick. Joules's handlebars hit a patch of mortar, which crumbled to dust and fell into the weeds at her feet. The giant smokestack that jutted from the center of the building tilted perilously and looked as if it might fall at any moment. Weeds pushed up through the cracks that snaked across the asphalt parking lot. The decaying factory was losing the battle against nature, which crept up from the river and would soon overtake everything that wasn't stone, and much of what was. The factory was like a creepy ghost town, so depressing that even the ghosts left.

A dense mass of brambles and brush surrounded the factory and stretched deep into the woods. Kevin pointed north toward the shadowy forest.

"The paper said the rocket crashed up there through the woods," he said.

"We have to find a rabbit first," said Joules. "Let's go this way."

Joules pointed her hiking stick toward the back of the factory.

Going "this way" was not Kevin's first choice. He preferred exploring "right here." There was much to see in the parking lot before running around a corner where anything could be hiding. Kevin had seen enough movies on *The Late, Late, Late Creepy Show for Insomniacs* to know that some places should always be avoided if you don't want to end up like the first character in a movie to die a gruesome death. In fact, Kevin kept a chart in his notebook for this very purpose and made a mental note to add "Abandoned tissue factory" to the list.

It did not matter that Kevin wanted to stay in one spot for a few minutes. Joules was already running toward the back corner of the factory. And as Kevin also knew, the only thing worse than running "that way" when someone said "Let's go" was *not* running "that way" when someone said "Let's go."

Joules disappeared around the crumbling brick corner. Kevin gripped his puny butterfly net like a baseball bat and ran after her.

KEVIN'S CHART OF PLACES TO AVOID

PLACE	MOVIE	WHAT HAPPENS THERE
Big old houses with creaky porches and rocking chairs	*Don't Look Under the Porch* *Rocking Chair Monster* *That's Not Your Grandma!*	The old lady you think is going to give you cookies and be nice to you ends up being really, *really* not nice to you and not giving you cookies, either.
Cemeteries, crypts, and morgues	Every movie ever	These places are filled with dead people. And if these places are in movies, it means the dead people aren't as dead as they should be. What do you think is going to happen?
The ocean	*Squidface* *Clownfish of Death* *Sharkapalooza* *Night of the Living Sea Cucumbers*	Everything in the ocean exists to eat people. If something in the ocean hasn't eaten a person yet, just wait. It will.
Deep space	*Lost in Deep Space* *Oh, Look, We're Still Lost in Deep Space* *How Deep Is This Deep Space?* *Bored to Death in Deep Space* *Attack of the Anything at All Would Be Nice at This Point in Deep Space* *Where Did Everyone Go?* *Hello? Hello? Anybody?* *Bueller? Bueller?* A million other movies about deep space	What is going to happen in deep space? Nothing. Why? Because there's nothing in deep space. That's why they call it deep space. It's nothing but space. The really, *really* deep kind. If there were cows in deep space, it would be called cow space, and that's an udderly different thing altogether.

Chapter 13

Kevin ran around the corner of the factory and slammed into Joules, who had stopped abruptly. She elbowed him and pointed her stick down the narrow gap that ran between the crumbling brick wall and the dense brambles.

"Look!" she said.

Kevin looked where Joules was pointing, which was halfway to the far corner of the factory. A small gray creature huddled next to the crumbling wall. Kevin squeezed past Joules and tiptoed toward the creature, while Joules followed several feet behind him. (Any closer would have damaged her sense of smell.)

Kevin took three steps, then paused as the brush rustled behind him and sent a shiver down his spine. He took a few more steps and stopped three feet from the gray creature. Kevin raised his butterfly net.

Again, the brush rustled.

"What's that?" he whispered.

"It's the wind," said Joules.

Kevin raised a finger into the air.

"There isn't any wind," he said.

They listened carefully. Only the distant sound of a raven echoed through the still air.

Joules pointed her stick at the creature.

"Catch it and let's get out of here!"

Kevin took a step. Then another step. He raised his net, held his breath, and—**SWOOP!**

Kevin scooped the creature into his net and swung it high over his head. A round blue eyeball flew out of the net, bounced off Joules's cheek, and dropped to her feet.

"Aaaaah!" Joules screamed and jumped backward into a large, spiky bramble that jabbed her leg.

"Ouch!" she yelled, jerking her leg back.

Kevin snorted with laughter and reached into the net. He pulled out a dingy gray toy bunny with one missing eye.

"Not funny!" said Joules, punching Kevin in the arm.

"Want to bet?" asked Kevin, wiggling the moldy bunny in front of her face.

Joules grabbed the stuffed rabbit, hurled it into the brambles, and gave Kevin the stink-eye of all stink-eyes.

"Keep going," she said.

Kevin thought about saying something stupid like

"Eye-eye" or "Keep an eye out for more bunnies," but he knew better.

Kevin and Joules crept farther along the wall, past an exceptionally thick tangle of brambles. Just before the next corner of the factory, they found a mound of garbage with everything from soup cans to mildewed stuffed toys.

She poked her stick into the mound of trash. A cloud of dust burst into the air and—**FWOOSH!**

A small gray rabbit with an enormous nose burst out of the pile and hopped around the corner on its tiny feet.

"Get it!" yelled Joules.

Kevin ran around the corner, swinging his tiny butterfly net in front of him.

SWOOSH!

A giant, long-handled bass-fishing net scooped up the big-nosed rabbit in one smooth motion. Joules and Kevin rounded the corner just as the owner of the net jumped onto a blue bike and sped away.

"Woo-hoo!" yelled Mack Buckley. "Extra credit!"

As Mack rode away with the net over his shoulder, the rabbit inside stared back at the twins with swirly blue eyes.

"Get back here!" yelled Joules. "That's our rabbit!"

Mack was gone. Joules kicked the brick wall, sending a

shower of mortar dust flying into the air. The dust tickled Kevin's nose.

"Aaaaa-choo! Aaaaa-choo!"

Kevin pulled a pack of tissues from his backpack and blew his nose.

"Let's go home," said Joules.

"Aaaa-choo! Aaaa-choo!"

Joules did not wait for Kevin to finish his sneezing. She ran for the bikes at the front of the factory. Had she waited—had she even looked back at her sneezing brother—she might have noticed the very large, very rabbit-shaped shadow stretching over Kevin as he stood blowing his nose.

The large-nosed shadow rose up behind the boy. It stretched to twice Kevin's height. The shadow loomed behind him and raised its shadow-claws above Kevin's head. The shadow leaned closer and closer as Kevin squeezed his nose tight and blew—

Honk!

The shadow froze. Kevin blew his nose again.

Honk!

The shadow rabbit tilted its head back and forth, then grew taller. And taller. And taller still.

Kevin crumpled the tissue, tossed it to the ground, and ran after his sister.

As the putrid-smelling boy ran away, a now medium-sized rabbit, which had, until a moment ago, been quite small, hopped from behind the decaying wall of the factory, its enormous shadow dissolving away in the full sunlight. The rabbit drummed its tiny feet rapidly on the ground and sniffed the air with its large schnoz. It snagged the crumpled tissue with one razor-sharp claw and pressed the cool, damp tissue to its schnoz. It breathed in the lingering stench as it watched the boy disappear beyond the edge of the factory. The rabbit dropped the tissue, flashed its fangs, and followed.

Chapter 14

The house was deserted when Kevin and Joules got home. Mr. and Mrs. Rockman were on their weekly SPAM shopping trip. Joules sank into a kitchen chair and gulped down an icy glass of water.

"We need to get cooking," Joules said.

"Good," said Kevin. "I'm starving. That was a long ride."

"We're not cooking dinner," said Joules.

Kevin knew that Joules wasn't talking about dinner. She was talking about splurp. Splurp was a special and highly toxic combination of nastiness that they had invented in the kitchen of an abandoned NASA facility near Camp Whatsitooya. It was a nauseating purplish-greenish-brownish goop with the power to neutralize the band of Fierce, Large, Ugly, and Ferocious Furballs that had taken over the camp and had threatened to take over the whole planet.

"We shouldn't do that," said Kevin, who was exhausted and just wanted to eat and take a shower. He was too tired to spend the next three hours mixing up a brew nasty enough to fight aliens.

"Besides, we don't know enough yet," he reasoned. "We might not need it. These might just be really ugly bunnies."

"Look me straight in the eye and tell me these are just really ugly bunnies," said Joules. "Besides, their eyes are the same."

"I know," said Kevin, "but we don't have any evidence that splurp will affect them at all. We need to study them."

Kevin flipped open his notebook and looked at a drawing he'd made of the Fluffs they had encountered at camp.

"They don't look like these rabbits from camp," he said. "We need a chart to help figure this out."

"Their eyes look the same," said Joules. "I don't know if splurp will work on them if they go alien-crazy on everyone, but we need to be prepared. Just in case."

"Maybe we need to do both," said Kevin.

"Okay," said Joules. "You make a chart. I'll get the SPAM."

Joules pulled out the soup pot and raided the pantry. She pulled out six cans of SPAM, that delicious canned meat that her parents were famous for using in their recipes. Mr. and Mrs. Rockman adored SPAM. In fact, the Rockmans were the reigning SPAM King and SPAM Queen at the International SPAMathon in Cheekville, Pennsylvania.

But wait! Those of you who were paying attention to the first paragraph of this chapter will remember that the Rockmans were out buying SPAM. Why would they do that when they clearly had cans of the delicious cubed meat in their cupboard? Here's why. Because you can't have too much SPAM. Truly. It is not possible.

THE CORNERSTONE TO EVERY SQUARE MEAL.

Those of you who didn't notice that the Rockmans were out buying SPAM when they already had some should pay more attention. Really! Paying attention helps build stronger brains. (This message was brought to you by your English teacher, who—it should be said—is getting a little tired of spending a teacher's income to pay for commercials and offer bribes. English teachers work hard. They care deeply about your education. But they do not get paid in gold doubloons. Perhaps if your school district started paying in gold doubloons, things would be different. But it doesn't. So until it does, be grateful you have such a caring English teacher and pay attention!)

When suddenly . . . we stopped talking about your English teacher and got back to the story! Joules opened the SPAM and drained the juice into the soup pot. For good measure, she tossed in a few chunks of meat to help the brew. She raided the fridge and added all kinds of things she could not identify—which was almost everything—and a few that she could: ketchup, mustard, mushroom soup, prune juice, Trix cereal, pickles, peanut butter, hot sauce . . .

As the concoction simmered, lovely sweet and flowery aromas filled the room. Aromas that reminded Joules of a sunny spring day filled with blooming flowers.

Ha! That was a lie. And if your spring days smell like Joules's concoction, you might consider moving.

Soon, the concoction plopped and splurped and turned the color of the tile in a campground shower.

"I think it's done," said Joules.

"Me too," said Kevin.

Joules turned off the burner and looked at Kevin's chart.

"That about sums it up," she said.

"Yep," said Kevin. "Pass the splurp."

WHAT WE KNOW	WHAT WE NEED TO FIND OUT BEFORE IT IS TOO LATE
Almost nothing	Everything else

Chapter 15

When suddenly . . .

Joules and Kevin Rockman once more entered the front doors of TBD School. Actually, while this seems very sudden to you, it was not at all sudden to them. Seventeen hours had passed since they had left school. During those hours, the Rockman twins had visited the Snottie's Tissue Factory, returned home, cooked up a batch of splurp, and filled two large spray bottles, which they stuck inside their backpacks. After that, they ate dinner, went to bed, got up, got dressed, and returned to school. Phew! They were busy!

Now that you know all these things, their being back at school probably does not seem sudden to you, either. Perhaps we should start again.

When finally . . .

Joules and Kevin Rockman once more entered the front doors of TBD School. As always, they were greeted by Principal Posner and her band of too-slow-to-avoid-being-bandaged-up students.

A first-grade girl entering just before the twins sneezed as she passed the principal.

"Into your elbow!" yelled the principal. "Always sneeze into your elbow! Are you trying to contaminate everyone?"

The stunned girl paused and dutifully raised her elbow to her nose. Principal Posner jumped into action. Within seconds the girl was bandaged head to toe with her bent arm wrapped securely over her face. She looked like a triangle-headed mummy.

"Four-point-five seconds," Principal Posner said proudly, admiring her work.

As Joules and Kevin quickly slipped past her, Joules bumped into a tall mummy with red high-top sneakers.

"Mmmmmm," groaned the mummy.

"Hey, Eric," said Joules.

"That's not Eric," said Kevin. "It's Elizabeth."

"Nope," said Joules, pointing at a girl by the lunchroom. "That's Elizabeth."

"Well, that's Eric over there," said Kevin.

"Whatever," said Joules.

Joules and Kevin ducked into the biology room and took their seats at their usual lab table. They were not shocked to find Mack already sitting in his seat with his hand raised. Nor were they surprised to see a new cage on the floor containing the big-schnozzled gray rabbit he had snatched away from them at the factory.

However, they *were* surprised by something else. The first cage, which had been a small, square cage with a small rabbit only seventeen hours ago, was now a bulging metal orb crammed to the bursting point with a massive gray creature whose ragged fur poked through the cage's grille. The rabbit, which had been the size of a Chihuahua only seventeen hours earlier, had grown into a mangy, growling gray beast much bigger than a Chihuahua. It was now the size of a Chihuanard.

The rabbits pressed their faces against their cages. They wobbled their noses and sniffed the air hungrily while staring intensely at Kevin. Their blue eyes swirled while they drummed their tiny feet rapidly against the cage floors.

"They're creeping me out," he whispered to Joules.

"I think they like you," said Joules. "Maybe it's your smell."

"What? I smell?" Kevin asked. "That's not possible. I showered when we got home from the factory! How do I smell?"

"Bad?" suggested Joules, scooting away.

"No way!" said Kevin.

"Ooh!" said Joules. "I just remembered I need to sit up there."

She swooped up her books and sprinted to an empty seat at the front table. Kevin looked around to see if anyone was watching, then gave a sly sniff toward his shirt. It was no use. He was too stuffed up to tell if he smelled or not. He looked around again to see if anyone had seen him. As he turned, he noticed that the bowl of jala-sauer-fu he had dumped onto his pants the day before was now back on the counter and was filled to the brim with the green goop.

"Look!" Kevin yelled. "It's not me!"

"Keep telling yourself that!" said Joules, making a sour face and pinching her nose shut.

"Funny," said Kevin.

At that moment, Mr. H came in, hung his coat over Mack's raised hand, and sat down without noticing the students.

Joules and Kevin breathed a sigh of relief. Mr. H was safe. Most people would not be worried about Mr. H. After all, he was a grown man capable of running away if something frightened him. But Joules and Kevin knew better. Mr. H, like their parents, did not find the unknown frightening. They found it thrilling. They were curious about everything and sought answers to all the questions they encountered. It's what made them scientists. It also made them forget that sometimes the unknown can be interesting *and* deadly.

Chapter 16

After twenty minutes, Mr. H looked up, freaked out about the short freshmen staring at him, and finally began class for real. His lecture was "Thermochemical Properties of Albumen and Protein Emulsions and the—"

Hey!

Wake up!

You were dozing off. It's true that chemistry can be challenging, but it won't help if you fall asleep. Now, where were we . . . Oh yeah . . .

Mr. H's lecture was "Thermochemical Properties of Albumen and Protein Emulsions and the Diffusion Rate of Glucose and 3-carboxy-3-hydroxypentanedioic Acid Molecules in Dihydrogen Monoxide Solution."

Phew! That was a mouthful. Okay. Take a quick nap if you need to recover. We'll wait.

. . . .
. . . .
. . . .
. . . .

. . . .
. . . .
. . . .
. . . .
. . . .
. . . . la la la la . . . . La la la la . . . .
LA LA LA LA . . . . LA! LA! LA! LA! . . . . . LA! LA!
LA! LA! . . . . . Oh. We're sorry. Did our singing wake you?
Well, now that you're up, let's continue!

Mr. H hummed as he danced around the class, pulling items from the cabinets and performing a series of experiments. He reached into the tiny refrigerator on the counter behind his desk and pulled out a glass beaker filled with a gloppy yellow liquid. He rapidly whisked the mixture until it frothed, then poured it into a metal pan over an electric hot plate. He was happy as a clam. He asked Joules to assist.

"Please stir this," he said, handing a wooden spoon to Joules.

She stirred the yellow liquid, which instantly clumped together.

"Wait a minute," Joules said. "Are we making scrambled eggs?"

"We are making science!" said Mr. H gleefully.

He opened a can of frozen orange juice and dumped it into a flask of water. He stirred it with a long glass rod.

"Watch those molecules diffuse!" he said.

He reached into his briefcase, pulled out a piece of bread, a pair of tongs, and laboratory goggles. He lit a Bunsen burner and stuck the bread over the flame.

"Wait until you see tomorrow's lesson!" he said, pulling a giant bag of potatoes from a cabinet and dropping it on the counter. Before Mr. H could describe the next day's lecture—"Methods to Preserve the Structure of Fragile Polysaccharide Molecules in a Lactose Infusion of Common Fatty Acids—Or, How to Make Great Mashed Potatoes"—the bell rang.

As the other students packed up to leave, Kevin walked over to Joules and Mr. H.

"Have you noticed how big and weird that rabbit looks now?"

Mr. H arched his eyebrows and looked over his round glasses. He gave Kevin a kind but nudging look.

"Remember our lesson from yesterday, Kevin?" he asked. "That is an Other. If it flew, we would reclassify it. But that has not flown. Has it?"

"Well, no," Kevin said. "But look at it! It's massive and it has fangs and—"

"Kevin," said Mr. H with a wink. "You watch too many movies. You should try looking at the world in an organized way like your sister! Try taking better notes in class. Now, off you go."

"Yeah, Kevin," said Joules. "You should try using a notebook sometime. They're the best."

Kevin rolled his eyes at his sister, who stuck her tongue out at him when Mr. H turned around to scoop some of his experiment onto a plate. He squirted some "red emulsion," which you might recognize as ketchup, onto his eggs and sat down to eat. The conversation was over.

Kevin shook his head. Mr. H was a brilliant man, but even brilliant people get things all wrong sometimes. At least Mr. H was safe. Though as Kevin walked by the rabbits, which growled softly at him, he wondered if anyone would remain safe for long.

Chapter 17

The rest of the day passed slowly until gym class, when time came to a complete screeching halt thanks to the president of the United States. Well, thanks to *a* president of the United States. The one a long time ago who decided to test how many sit-ups, push-ups, and—worst of all—pull-ups kids could do. Millions of American schoolchildren have taken the President's Physical Fitness Test throughout the years. It was the President's Physical Fitness Test that inspired Mr. Shhh to create the Noodle-Armor and become a bazillionaire. Most people who have taken the President's Physical Fitness Test have not become bazillionaires. Or even millionaires. Or even hundredaires. They have become tired and cranky. Kevin was no exception. Each year, the test was a disaster. To say that he hated it would be a ridiculous understatement.

Nobody actually remembers which president started the President's Physical Fitness Test, but Kevin had a sneaking suspicion it was Rutherford B. Hayes. He had a shifty look about him.

Since Kevin was forbidden to have his notebook during the test, he made a mental note to create a list of suspicious presidents. It would include a president named Grover, who had starred on *Sesame Street* but later denied it, and Martin Van Buren, who used his bushy sideburns to smuggle food and small animals into the White House.

One by one, Kevin's classmates approached the bar fastened to the gym wall at a height of six feet. They jumped up and grabbed the bar, then did a series of pull-ups, counting as they went: eleven . . . twelve . . . thirteen . . .

After a respectable number, but before their arms fell off, each kid dropped from the bar and walked off, rubbing their arms and smiling. Joules did seventeen pull-ups. She could have done more, but Stinkbomb McGee was in line after her, so her oxygen supply was limited. Stinkbomb McGee got his name in third grade after he stole his teenage brother's stash of body spray and used a whole can on one armpit. The cologne cloud that surrounded him led to an unexpected "field trip" for the school, during which all the students spent the day in the field next to the school. It was soggy. It was filled with mosquitoes. But the air was lovely.

After a long talk with the school nurse about personal hygiene, Stinkbomb cut back to one can per day for his whole body. After that, the cologne cloud that surrounded Stinkbomb shrank from one block to only three feet. Since the nurse did not get within three feet of Stinkbomb, she considered the problem solved. Everyone else learned to hold their breath.

Living in a bubble of body spray had a surprising effect on Stinkbomb. Much like people who live at very high altitudes with low oxygen levels, he developed very efficient lungs. He also became very strong. Stinkbomb easily did thirty-six pull-ups before he got bored and quit.

Kevin was next. He approached the bar and took a deep breath of lingering body spray, which annoyed his stuffed-up nose and made him sneeze. Kevin raised his arms and was about to jump up and grab the bar above his head when—**SFLOMP!**—Mr. Shhh slapped a pair of nylon bands around Kevin's upper arms and fastened them shut with Velcro. Noodle-Armor. Each band was attached to a purple bungee cord, which Mr. Shhh hooked to the pull-up bar, lifting Kevin two feet off the floor in the process.

"This will fix those noodle arms!" said Mr. Shhh, pulling Kevin's feet toward the floor and stretching the bungees to their limit.

"But I don't want—"

"Grab the bar on your way up!" said the gym teacher. "You'll thank me when you have arms like these!"

TWANGGGGG.

Mr. Shhh let go of Kevin's feet and struck a bodybuilder pose, showing off his bulging biceps. Kevin did not notice. He was too busy screaming and flying straight toward the bar and then right past it. He shot upward until his head was two feet above the bar. While the air that high up was free of body spray, Kevin did not have time to notice or breathe. He was too busy screaming.

HEEEEEEEEEEEEEEELP!!!!!!"......

Chapter 18

"WHOAAAAAAAAAA!!!!!!"

Kevin screamed as the bungees stretched to their maximum length. His ascent slowed and he stopped for one heartbeat, before hurtling toward the floor with terrifying speed. He plunged toward the ground until his tiptoes touched the floor and he stopped for one instant. Then—**TWANG**—Kevin shot up again. Up and down and up and down . . . Kevin bounced through the air like a kangaroo on a trampoline. He missed the bar on his way back down . . . and back up . . . and back down . . . and back . . . Well, you get the idea . . .

AAAAAAAAAAAAAAAHAHAHAHHHHHHHHHHHHHHHH

Kevin's classmates stopped their push-ups and sit-ups and counted his attempts to grasp the bar as he zoomed past . . . Twelve! . . . Thirteen! . . . Fourteen! . . . When suddenly . . .

BAM!

A loud noise echoed through the halls of the school. The crowd of students watching Kevin, including Joules, ran into the hall to see what was going on.

Joules looked down the hall and saw a tall, unfamiliar woman dressed in purple. The woman had blond hair, square glasses, and a very large nose. The woman pushed her way through the excited crowd of students, turned the corner, and disappeared.

"Waiiiiaaaaiiiiiaaaaiiiiitttttt!" Kevin yelled.

Joules did not wait. She elbowed her way into the crowd and—

CRASH!

The students surged toward the noises, sweeping Joules along in their current to the biology room. They rounded the corner and stopped. The hallway outside Mr. H's classroom was littered with broken chair bits. The group pushed into the room, which looked as if a tornado had ripped through it. Chairs were knocked over; textbooks and broken glassware littered the floor. Next to Mr. H's desk sat the remains of two empty metal cages, which had been blown to shreds.

"Stand back!" yelled Mr. Shhh, jumping in front of Joules. "This is a job for someone with arms like these!"

He pumped first one bicep, then the other. The students applauded.

"They are impressive, aren't they?" said Mr. Shhh, making his biceps pop up and down. "Wow! This is a mess. Whoever did that had some very impressive arms indeed. They must use the Noodle-Armor!"

He struck a new pose and the students applauded again.

Joules knelt beside the destroyed cages and picked up a clump of greasy gray fur that smelled like the gunk at the bottom of her fish tank after a long vacation. A very long vacation. Mr. Shhh was wrong. The force that had torn the metal cages to shreds did not come from someone who used the Noodle-Armor. It had not come from a person at all. She picked up one of the curved metal fragments strewn across the floor. They had been blown apart by the force of the monsters inside them. Monsters that were now gone. A sick feeling hit Joules as she looked around the room and realized something much worse: Mr. H was gone, too.

Joules looked for Kevin among the students who stood applauding Mr. Shhh's biceps poses. He wasn't there. Joules ran back to the gym, where she expected to find Kevin suspended in the Noodle-Armor, yelling for help. Instead, she found a silent gym. The only sign that Kevin had been there was a shredded heap of nylon and Velcro that lay on the floor.

Joules scraped her fingernail over the Velcro and pulled away a wad of—you guessed it—fur. Greasy gray fur.

She stood up and looked around the empty gym.

"Kevin!" she yelled.

No answer.

She walked to the bleachers, unzipped her backpack, and pulled out a large spray bottle of splurp. She rezipped the compartment and tossed her backpack and Kevin's under the bleachers. She grabbed the spray bottle with her left hand and grabbed a lacrosse stick with her right, just as the bell rang. For the next thirty seconds, the halls were crammed with teachers and students racing for the exits. After one minute, the halls were empty.

"Okay, bunnies," said Joules, "you asked for it!"

Joules tested the spray bottle. A mist of stench filled the air and made her gag. She tightened her grip on the lacrosse stick and stepped into the hall. She hoped that Kevin was wrong and that the stinky concoction that lingered in the air would be enough to help her save her brother and Mr. H.

It had to be, she realized.

It was all she had.

Chapter 19

Joules's footsteps echoed down the halls of the empty school. Every few steps, she stopped, held her breath, and listened.

Silence.

Joules moved on quickly. Standing still was not her style. She searched hallway after hallway, stopping for only a heartbeat before jumping inside each classroom with her raised spray bottle of splurp and her lacrosse stick.

She had searched half the school and was just starting down the kindergarten hallway when suddenly . . .

Tlink. Tlink.

Joules stopped and listened. A faint noise echoed through the hall.

Tlink. Tlink.

Tlink. Tlink.

Joules followed the sound to Miss Bee's classroom. The door was open a few inches and she peeked inside. Miss Bee's room was the kind of overdecorated classroom Joules hated. The walls were plastered with construction-paper bees encouraging kids to "bee good" and "beehave" and "beeware of tooth decay." Miss Bee's boundless energy and sunny personality made her the perfect kindergarten teacher, even if her spelling was lacking. Clearly, Miss Bee took her name very seriously. She had a keen interest in flowers and yellow-and-black-striped clothing. She was as sweet as honey and busy as a—well, you know. Miss Bee flitted from student to student and from project to project, never stopping for long before buzzing off to the next thing. It was easy to imagine the classroom bustling with laughing children. Without them, the silent room had an eerie, sinister feeling.

Tlink. Tlink.

Tlink. Tlink.

Joules stepped into the empty room.

Tlink. Tlink.

She followed the sound to the yellow-and-black curtain stretched in front of the coat closet.

Tlink. Tlink.

I've got you now, she thought as she raised the spray bottle and stepped closer to the curtain, holding her breath.

"Ha!" she yelled, knocking the curtain back with the lacrosse stick and spritzing splurp into the closet.

The slimy juice splattered the glass wall of a terrarium,

where a fat brown toad stared blankly at her, stuck its tongue out, jumped full force against the glass, and fell back, knocking its water dish against the terrarium wall.

Tlink. Tlink.

Joules exhaled.

"Dumb toad," she said.

Joules grabbed a fistful of tissues from one of the dozens of boxes of Snottie's Tissues in the closet and wiped down the terrarium. The toad stuck out its tongue and jumped full force against the glass again.

Tlink. Tlink.

Tlink. Tlink.

Joules closed the closet curtain and went back to the hall. She leaned against a poster for the upcoming school chili supper and thought about Kevin. Where was he?

Tlink. Tlink.

Tlink. Tlink.

She followed the sound down the kindergarten class hallway and turned the corner and listened.

Tlink. Tlink.

The sound came from the lunchroom. Joules knew one thing about the lunchroom at TBD School. It might have a lot of very nasty food, but it did *not* have toads.

Chapter 20

Joules tightened her grip on the stick and tiptoed toward the lunchroom. The lunchroom at TBD School was a vast concrete-block room with folding tables that were pushed against the walls except at lunchtime. A large kitchen was connected to the lunchroom, and through that kitchen was a smaller kitchen, which had been the original kitchen when the school was built.

The lunchroom was empty. Only the sticky globs of lunch goop and the straws littering the floor showed that anyone had been there recently.

Tlink! Tlink!

The sound came from the kitchens.

Joules raised the spritzer and tiptoed into the big kitchen.

Tlink! Tlink!

Tlink! Tlink! Tlink!

Nobody was there. Along the far wall was an industrial drum labeled "SLAW." Joules had seen it many times. There was always a container like it at lunch. Normally,

Joules loved slaw. But she loved the good kind that people eat at lovely picnics along scenic rivers or in the shade of majestic mountains. This was military-grade slaw that Principal Posner got at a "super-great discount" from the local army base. Rumor had it that the slaw was used as a secret weapon by the military. It was not a very good secret. The slaw's smell could knock over a tank, and its sour power could strip paint from a jeep. Since TBD School did not have a tank, a jeep, or students foolish enough to eat the slaw, it lasted forever, which made it an even better bargain.

A mountain of empty tomato cans, chili sauce bottles, and five-gallon bean canisters rose up beside the industrial stove, where eight enormous brass cauldrons bubbled loudly. Their lids popped up every few seconds, spewing a cloud of steam into the air before settling back onto the cauldrons.

Tlink! Tlink! Tlink!

Joules tiptoed to the stove, leaned the stick against the wall, and lifted a lid from one of the cauldrons. A delicious cloud of chili vapor rose from the bubbling red brew. Chunks of meat, tomatoes, and beans bubbled to the surface, then sank again. It looked and smelled delightful.

Joules loved chili, and she especially loved the school's chili. It was the *only* thing she loved at school lunch, but it was very good. In fact, the chili was so good that the school's annual chili supper brought people from all over town and raised a lot of money for the school's Drum and Beagle Corps.

Many schools have a traditional Drum and Bugle Corps. As you know, they involve drums and bugles. However, the secretary at TBD goofed up on the invoice for equipment and ordered ten drums and thirty beagles. Since most people were afraid of the school secretary, they said nothing and a new tradition was born. The Drum and Beagle Corps was a mixed success. Everyone loved the beagles. The beagles, however, did *not* love the drums and ran away each time someone hit the bass drum. (Which, as it turned out, was during every song.) The school quickly started the chili supper to pay for dog food and replacement beagles.

Joules put the lid back on the first pot and lifted the lid from another. She leaned close and sniffed. A horrible stench bubble burst into the air two inches from her face and made her gag. She dropped the lid, which clanged loudly on the concrete floor as the smell of swamp slime hit her in the face like a pie. A stink pie, that is. A stink pie made with slimy, oozy pond scum mixed with skunk juice.

Joules suddenly felt dizzy.

"Blech," she said, reaching for the lid.

She grabbed the lid and slammed it onto the bubbling cauldron.

"Girl student!"

Joules wheeled around and dropped the copper lid onto the floor, knocking over the lacrosse stick, which skidded out of reach over the smooth concrete.

"Why are you here?" asked Principal Posner, who stood only three feet away.

"Uh . . ."

Joules could not answer. She could only stare at the principal's nose. Her enormous bobbing schnozzle of a nose.

Chapter 21

"Principal Posner?"

"Who?" asked the bobbing-schnozzled figure. "Oh yes. That is a bad name. I am now Principal Grunt."

"Grunt?" asked Joules.

"That is my name," she said. "Do not wear it out."

Principal Posn—er, Grunt—stepped closer to Joules, who stepped back and raised the spray bottle.

"Get away," she said.

"Ha!" said Grunt, leaning forward.

Joules backed up toward the entrance of the small kitchen. Grunt smiled, revealing very sharp teeth.

"You are nosy," said Grunt. "I should know what nosy looks like! Ha ha ha! I am funny."

She stepped toward Joules, who backed into the small kitchen. Again, Grunt stepped closer and closer and Joules moved back and back and . . .

CRASH!

Joules slammed into an enormous metal tube dangling from a huge contraption standing in the middle of the kitchen.

"Wha—?"

"Do you like our invention?" asked Grunt, her schnoz wobbling faster.

Joules looked at the tangled mess of metal and plastic pipes jutting out from a three-wheeled tank that looked like a fat water heater with a motor. A showerhead tied to a hockey stick with dirty tube socks dangled above everything.

"What is that?" asked Joules.

"This is the machine that will bring the human race to its knees!" said a voice from behind the contraption.

A triangular man with huge biceps and an enormous wobbly nose stepped out from behind the weird machine. His nose wobbled up and down as he sniffed the air. He stamped his tiny feet rapidly on the floor.

"Humans are weak and silly!"

"Mr. Shhh?"

"Do not say 'shhh' to me!" said Mr. Shhh. "I am Captain Belcher."

"Belcher?" asked Joules. "Where is Mr. Shhh?"

"Ha!" said Belcher. "That gym man thought he was strong. He did this, but it did not save him."

He struck a pose, flexed his biceps, and glared at Joules as his eyes began to swirl faster and faster. He stamped his puny feet rapidly on the concrete floor. He moved closer to Joules. A putrid odor hit her and she gasped.

"Blech! Get back!" she said.

Spritz! Spritz!

Joules sprayed Belcher squarely in the schnoz.

He paused for a moment and breathed it in. He sighed happily. Breathed in again and stretched . . . No, he did not stretch. Right before Joules's eyes, Captain Belcher grew six inches taller.

"That was delicious," he said, grabbing at the spray bottle. "Give me that."

"I want some!" said Grunt, inhaling deeply.

"Yum!" she said. "So much power! Just what I need after our long journey!"

"The Earthlings contain no power, but they are a crunchy snack," said Belcher. "The gym teacher tasted like gym socks. I like gym socks, but they are not good food."

"That principal lady was not tasty," said Grunt. "She tasted like bandages. Blech."

"Are you a good snack?" asked Belcher, leaning close to Joules, who tried to look away—but it was too late.

Belcher's swirly eyes pulled her closer. Suddenly, Joules felt weak. She wanted to run. She needed to run. And yet, she could not move. Joules dropped the spray bottle and Grunt dived for it, knocking Belcher over.

For a heartbeat, Belcher broke eye contact and Joules could move. Her mind was hazy and she imagined she heard a distant voice calling her through a dense fog. Joules stumbled for the door.

"Ha! Run away, silly Earth person!" yelled Grunt. "We like your smelly planet with the soft tissues, and we will rule it! Tomorrow we will have all the power we need!"

"Ha ha! Earth student," yelled Belcher. "Run away. Our machine will give us the power to control you all! Give me that bottle."

SMACK!
Whap!
Slap!
Crash!

Joules ran down the hall, followed by the sound of angry laughter and a deafening **BAM**-Crash-**Slap**-**Whap**-**SMACK**down.

She turned the corner, and—

BAM!

She slammed full force into a mummy and fell to the floor. The mummy ricocheted from wall to wall down the empty hall.

"MMMMMMMM!!!!"

Joules looked at the mummy's faded black sneakers. Faded black sneakers exactly like a pair she had seen every day. Faded black sneakers that could only belong to—

"Kevin?"

"Mmmmmm!"

Joules got up and ran to the mummy. She jerked a strand of gauze dangling from the mummy's back, sending her brother spinning down the hall like a human top. His bandages fell away as he ricocheted off the wall again and landed in a dizzy heap on the floor.

"We have to get out of here!" yelled Joules.

She pulled Kevin up by the hand and raced to the door at the end of the hall.

They burst out of the school and stumbled into the bright sunlight of the playground. Kevin steadied himself and blinked.

"Thanks for the rescue," he said.

"We're not safe yet," said Joules. "Nobody is safe."

Kevin did not have to ask his sister to explain. He did not need to. One look at her face told him that they were in trouble. Big, hairy, stinky trouble.

Chapter 22

The twins cut through the field behind the playground and let themselves into the house. They dropped onto the couch and sat for a moment, catching their breath.

"Where did you go?" asked Joules.

"Everybody ran out of the gym and left me bouncing up and down in that stupid thing and I couldn't get out," said Kevin. "I finally stopped bouncing all over the place when it attacked me!"

"The Noodle-Armor attacked you?"

"No!" said Kevin. "The gigantic alien rabbit ripped me out of the Noodle-Armor and tried to eat me alive. I only got away because I kicked it right in the schnoz and it dropped me. I ran, and I was almost out of the school when the principal wrapped me up."

"She won't be doing that anymore," said Joules.

"What do you mean?"

"We have a new principal," said Joules. "Her name is Grunt."

"Oh," said Kevin. "What are we going to do?"

"We're going to take a page out of your book," said Joules. "It's research time, and I know exactly where to start."

"I'll get a notebook," said Kevin.

"I'll get a stick."

Five minutes later, the Rockman twins were biking toward the old Snottie's Tissue Factory outside town. As they rode, Joules told Kevin about Principal Grunt and Captain Belcher and the contraption in the kitchen. They biked past the factory and turned onto a gravel road that led across the river. The road curved into the forest that marked the official end of town. A few hundred yards into the woods, the road was blocked by a set of barricades with an enormous, official-looking sign:

"Looks like we're in the right place," said Kevin.

Joules and Kevin rode around the barricades and continued down the road to a spot where the weeds had been trampled flat and a narrow footpath veered into the forest.

They dropped their bikes at the edge of the road and stepped into the deep shade of the forest. As they stepped deeper and deeper into the shadows, they could not help remembering a similar path in the deep forests of Camp Whatsitooya last summer. Neither spoke as they walked into the dark woods.

Eventually, the path reached a fresh clearing in the woods created by something that had crashed through the forest canopy and wiped out the trees in a gigantic circle. One thing was clear about the clearing. It had clearly not been a clearing for very long. Is that clear? Clearly.

It was also clear that the thing that had crushed all the trees now sat at the center of the clearing wrapped in yellow hazard tape. Turn the page to see what that thing looked like.

Joules and Kevin climbed through the broken hatch and into the battered rocket. They had been in a rocket like this before, but that rocket was burned out and rusted. This one was crumpled but intact. Joules waved her hand in front of her nose as a putrid stench hit her square in the face.

"This stinks like that nasty goop on the stove at school," said Joules.

"It stinks like the alien who grabbed me," said Kevin.

Kevin made a note while Joules randomly pushed buttons on the control panel. A little door near the hatch popped open, revealing a narrow strip of photographs.

"It's a photo booth!" said Kevin.

It was indeed, and on the next page is what the strip showed.

Chapter 23

Have you ever wondered how they find volunteers to test the parachutes? Neither have we. Gee, it's nice that we think alike, isn't it?

Chapter 24

When suddenly . . . the point of that last chapter escaped us entirely. We hate it when that happens. But it doesn't matter. What matters is that Joules and Kevin searched the rocket for anything that might help them stop the killer rabbits.

"There's nothing here," said Kevin. "Let's—"

Snap!

"Shh!" whispered Joules, raising a hand to silence her brother.

Crack!

"Someone's out there," whispered Kevin.

"Shh!"

Joules grabbed a jar of Tang and stepped toward the door.

"What are you—" Kevin began.

Snap!

"Ha!" Joules jumped out of the hatch and hurled the jar toward the noise.

WHOOSH!

A fat gray squirrel jumped from a log, where it had been eating an acorn. The jar crashed against the log, exploding into an orange cloud of dust. The squirrel scurried up a nearby tree and chattered angrily at Joules.

"Stupid squirrel," Joules said. "Let's—"

SNAP!

Joules turned just in time to see a dark purple figure slip into the forest and disappear into the shadows.

Chapter 25

That night, Kevin completed his chart of things they knew and things they needed to find out before it was too late. It was hard to know if the chart would help them with a plan, but it made Kevin feel better. He had made a similar chart at Camp Whatsitooya when they encountered the Fierce, Large, Ugly, and Ferocious Furballs, and it had helped. He hoped this one would, too.

We could show you the chart Kevin made at summer camp, but that would be like showing you last week's TV schedule. Boring and not useful. Instead, we will show you this week's TV schedule and Kevin's new chart.

WHAT WE KNOW	WHAT WE NEED TO FIND OUT BEFORE IT IS TOO LATE
• A rocket crashed outside of town.	• Where is Mr. H?
• The rocket was created by E.A.R.S.—an organization from NASA.	• Where is the 3rd alien?
• The rocket contained 3 helmets.	• What does the machine do?
• 3 helmets = 3 passengers = 3 aliens = trouble	• How does it control people?
• The gym teacher + the principal = 1 missing alien	• How do we stop them?
• They built a contraption.	• CAN they be stopped?
• They will use it to control people and take over the world.	
• They are ugly.	
• Their eyes are hypnotic.	
• Smell makes them grow very fast.	
• They smell VERY, VERY bad.	

Ha! We tricked you. We did not show you this week's TV schedule. Your English teacher bribed us to tell you to work on your spelling instead of watching TV. We don't know why. We thinck yur speeling iz phine.

Joules and Kevin sat at the kitchen table staring at the chart. It had been an hour since they'd added anything new to the list, and they had no idea what to do next.

"Do you think we'll see Mr. H again?" asked Kevin.

The look Joules gave him was all the answer he needed.

Kevin quietly closed his notebook and took it to his room. He stuck the notebook and pen beneath his pillow in case he thought of a plan in the middle of the night. Then he took a shower and went to bed early. Joules also went to bed early, but it was many hours before either slept. They could not stop thinking about Kevin's chart of things they knew and things they needed to find out before it was too late.

As they each lay awake in their dark rooms, a deep dread in their hearts told them that it already was.

Chapter 26

The next morning, Joules awoke to the nasty smell of breakfast. Instead of being annoyed as usual, she was overjoyed at the smell. It was nothing compared to the toxic fumes in the school kitchen the day before, and she was just glad to know that her family was safe.

Kevin handed her a newspaper as she dropped into her seat at the table.

"Read that," he said.

Continued from page 1A

who explained the use of advertisements on the rockets. "With budget cuts, we need the money," he said. "We've had great results and we must keep this important work going."

Professor Dewdy also commented that...Oh wait...His name sounds like doody...HEE HEE HEE. HA! What were his parents thinking? Seriously? That was just silly!...

While she read, Joules zoned out the conversation in the kitchen, but she zoned back in when Kevin slammed his hand on the table.

"You guys can't go!" he said angrily. "You and Mom have to stay home."

"Nonsense," said Mr. Rockman, stirring a pot of something blue, juicy, and very smelly. "We never miss the chili supper. Their recipes could use some excitement—and SPAM—but it's important to support the school."

"It's canceled," said Kevin.

"Also nonsense," said Mrs. Rockman, tossing a handful of garlic into the bubbling blue liquid. "They would never cancel the chili supper. How else would the Drum and Beagle Corps afford dog food? We have errands after work, and we will meet you at the school."

"No!" said Joules. "There are three killer aliens with enormous schnozzes at the school. They have already eaten the principal and the gym teacher."

She paused.

"They want to take over the world."

Mrs. Rockman burst into laughter and hugged Joules tightly.

"You two make us laugh so hard," she said, wiping a tear from her eye. "We do love you!"

Joules looked at Kevin, who shook his head.

Mrs. Rockman chuckled as she went to the fridge and pulled a bowl of green stuff from the shelf. While Mr. and Mrs. Rockman debated whether to add the green stuff to the smelly blue goo, Kevin and Joules sneaked out the back door. They were not surprised that their parents had laughed. It was the reason Joules and Kevin hadn't already called the police or the FBI or a friendly old neighbor. Nobody would believe this story. The twins had seen enough movies on *The Late, Late, Late Creepy Show for Insomniacs* to know that. Joules and Kevin knew that it was up to them—and them alone—to stop the aliens.

"So what are we going to do?" asked Kevin.

"The only thing we can do," said Joules. "Improvise!"

Kevin walked slowly, trying desperately to come up with a new plan before they reached the school. He did not like this plan, but he did not have a better one. Perhaps you should think of a plan. If you succeed, please let the twins know ASAP. Really. Get a ride to their school and go tell them right now. You will need a ride unless you can drive yourself. If you can . . . Wow! That is really cool. How did you get a license? Do you have your own car? Really? Does it get good mileage? You *are* lucky. Now get going! And buckle up. And pick up some cake on your way back. We're hungry.

If you do not have a great plan (or a car), don't feel bad. Coming up with a great plan is harder than it looks. Consider one of the best plans ever. It was created by Hannibal during the Second Punic War (not to be confused with the First Puny War, which was no big deal). During the Second Punic War, the Carthaginians and the Romans had a nasty spat going until a man from Carthage named Hannibal marched a lot of men and thirty-seven elephants over the Alps and surprised everyone. Especially the elephants, who thought they were going to the circus. The Carthaginians lost many soldiers during that trek, but they won the battle and changed the course of history.

Now, consider Hannibal's brother, Sam, who had a different plan to surprise the Romans. Sam strapped himself to a dolphin and tried to ram a Roman ship full of laughing sailors while throwing melons at them. Sadly, the dolphin brushed Sam off in a patch of kelp. He washed up onshore with a mouthful of seaweed and sand in his pants. When mocked for his plan, Sam defended it, saying that eating seaweed and stuffing his pants with sand was his plan all along. Historians agree. After all, he did it on porpoise.

Chapter 27

When suddenly . . . we regretted that porpoise joke. Honestly. Everyone knows that dolphins and porpoises are two completely different animals. Though as you also know, both are Others, since they cannot fly. This doesn't matter. What matters is that Joules and Kevin were about to enter the school and battle aliens. So let's get back to that before they change their minds and stay home, leaving the fate of Earth in question and the remaining pages of this book empty. Nobody wants that.

Especially not the publisher.

Chapter 28

The twins reached the front door of TBD School.

"Ready?" Joules asked.

"Nope."

"Me neither."

Joules pushed open the door.

Principal Posner and her band of freshly wrapped mummies were not at the entrance of the school as usual. There was only one mummy in the crowd of incoming students. A third grader bumped the mummy with her shoulders and sent it ricocheting down the hall like a rubber ducky bouncing against the boulders of a white-water river. The mummy bounced against Kevin.

"Mmmmmm!"

"Can't talk now, Caedence," said Kevin.

"Mmmmmm."

The mummy banged into Joules, who bumped it with her shoulder and sent it ricocheting back through the crowd.

"Mmmmmmmmmmmmmm!"

"Meg can be so annoying," said Joules.

"That wasn't Meg," said Kevin, pointing at a red-haired girl tying her shoe. "Meg is over there."

"Whatever," said Joules.

"Let's get to class," said Kevin. "Maybe Mr. H will be there."

"I hope so," said Joules. "But what if he went looking for the rocket or more of the bunnies? You know how Mr. H is. He could walk right into disaster and never notice."

Kevin nodded.

Mr. H was not in the biology room. Joules and Kevin took their seats and watched the clock nervously, hoping that he was just late. After a few moments, the door opened and a balding middle-aged man dressed like William Shakespeare entered. He waltzed dramatically to the front of the classroom, struck a pose beside the desk, and addressed the class in a bogus Olde English accent. (The "e" at the end proves that it is very olde.)

"Hark and lo, what light through yonder window breaks?" he said. "'Tis but I, Sir John Gilbad, your lowly servant and substitute educator for the day."

He paused and looked expectantly at the class. They stared at him blankly.

He took a bow and stood up again.

"Bravo!" yelled Mack, standing and clapping vigorously.

The substitute smiled and bowed again.

"A grant of ten extra-credit points to ye, kinde sir," said Sir John.

"Woo-hoo!" shouted Mack.

"Where is Mr. H?" asked Kevin. "Will he be here today?"

The substitute climbed onto the desk and dramatically thrust his arms into the air.

"To be here or *not* to be here," he said. "That is the question."

Clearly, the answer was "not."

Sir John stood upon Mr. H's desk, adjusted his floppy velvet cap, and began his musical rendition of Shakespeare's *Romeo and Juliet*, in which he played Romeo *and* Juliet *and* Hamlet *and* Macbeth *and* a guy named Henry V who was in a big war that lasted a hundred years. Joules suspected it would feel like a thousand years by the time class ended.

She nudged Kevin and pointed toward the door. Silently, they got up and headed for the door. Sir John stopped mid-song.

"Wherefore art thou goest?" he asked. "Ye will miss the big musical number. I wrote it myself!"

He picked up a fake skull and sang, "Alas, poor Yorick. What a fella. Just a skull that's old and yella."

Mack clapped again. Joules rolled her eyes.

"Uh . . . ," said Kevin. "We're going to . . . uh . . ."

"We're going to go tell everyone about your show!" said Joules.

"Then make haste!" said Sir John. "For all the world's a stage, and all the men and women merely players. They have their exits and their—"

Click.

Joules and Kevin ducked into the hallway and pulled the door closed behind them. They ran down the hall, followed by the faint sounds of tap dancing and applause.

Chapter 29

Joules and Kevin ran to the cafeteria. The lunch tables, which had been folded against the walls the night before, were now unfolded and spaced neatly from one wall to the other. A set of carts with lunch trays, bowls, plates, silverware, and—of course—ketchup lined the east wall. Every lunch at TBD School involved ketchup. Even when the meal was cereal. Don't ask.

Kevin and Joules stepped into the lunchroom and tiptoed to the doorway of the big kitchen. The only evidence that anyone had been there was the chili cooking in two vats on the stove.

The twins listened carefully. They heard only the sound of burbling chili. They sneaked to the doorway of the small inner kitchen and peeked inside. Again, the only evidence that anyone had been there was another giant pot of bubbling chili and a mound of discarded tomato, bean, and chili sauce cans. There was no sign of the contraption or the aliens.

"What now?" asked Kevin.

"The gym," said Joules.

Thirty sweaty students were running laps around the gym when they arrived. A substitute teacher sat on the bleachers with her nose jammed into a paperback novel.

"Excuse me," said Kevin.

The substitute flipped a page and kept reading.

"Where is Mr. Shh—" said Joules.

"Shhh," said the teacher.

"Right," said Joules. "Where is Mr. Shhh?"

"Shhh."

"Well?" asked Joules. "Where is he?"

Without looking up, the substitute teacher waved her hand to dismiss them.

"Shhh."

"I think she means to be quiet," said Kevin.

The substitute flipped a page and kept reading.

"But—"

"Shhh."

They got the hint. Joules went to the end of the bleachers and pulled out their backpacks, which she had stashed the day before. They put on the packs and went to the aqua center.

TBD was the only school in town to have a pool, which

was a big deal even if it was not a big pool. When the school was built, the founders asked the architect to include an Olympic-sized pool. However, they failed to mention which Olympic sport they were interested in. They did not know that the architect was, in fact, a former Olympic Ping-Pong champion. He built a perfect Olympic (Ping-Pong table)-sized pool. This was great news for the swim team, which completed its hundred daily laps very quickly. It was horrible news for the kayaking class, because the pool held only one kayak. Every day, the entire kayak team piled into one kayak, which promptly sank and had to be fished out of the pool along with the team. Meanwhile, a dozen unused kayaks sat on a rack in the corner waiting for the day when they might be used. A day that never came.

However, while the pool was very small, the room in which it was placed was very large. The architect filled the aqua center with bleachers. Many, many, many—and can we emphasize *many*—bleachers. He dismissed the worry that having a thousand people staring at a pool the size of a Ping-Pong table might be a little weird by saying, "Yeah! So is your mother!" It was a point that few at TBD School could argue with, so the design remained.

There was nobody in the aqua center. It was cool inside. A giant air conditioner rumbled and pushed cold air through the enormous space.

The twins continued to the school office. The outer office had very large windows, which let the school secretary watch students walking down the halls, but kept them out of her way and—more importantly—out of her airspace, which was very important during cold season. The school secretary was not a fan of germs, or students for that matter.

Now the office blinds were lowered and a sign on the door read: "Go away."

Joules jiggled the door handle. It was locked.

"Joules," Kevin said.

Joules ignored him and jiggled the doorknob again.

"Joules . . ."

Joules banged on the door.

"Joules!" Kevin said. "Look at this."

"What?" she asked.

Kevin pointed to a poster taped to one corner of the office window. It was the same poster that was stuck to every wall in the school, announcing the chili supper, but someone had taken a black marker to it.

Joules read the poster and nodded.

"So now we know where and when they are going to make their move," said Joules.

"We just have to figure out what that move will be," said Kevin.

"There's only one way to find out," said Joules.

"I was afraid you'd say that," said Kevin.

Chapter 30

Joules and Kevin made it back to the biology room just as Sir John Gilbad finished his version of *King Lear* in mime. Their classmates stared with a horrified expression on their faces, their mouths dangling wide open. Only Mack stood and applauded.

"Why, thank thee, kind gentleman," said the substitute. "Again, sir, ten and five extra-credit points to ye."

The bell rang. Sir John Gilbad waved his hand toward the door.

"Once more unto the breach, dear friends, once more to your next classes!"

The dazed students gathered their books and stumbled out of the room. The twins headed to social studies, then math. After that, they went to lunch. As they walked down the halls, they counted fifteen chili supper posters scribbled on with the same message they had seen by the office. Someone had been busy during the last two hours.

The twins reached the lunchroom, ditched their backpacks at a corner table, and got in line behind a kid with a marked-up chili supper poster glued to his back. Someone had been very busy indeed.

When suddenly . . . Joules and Kevin looked up from the lunch line and into the face of a tall woman with square glasses, a dark purple shirt, and a very large schnoz.

Actually, this did not happen suddenly. It happened in the school cafeteria. Anyone who has ever been in a school cafeteria knows that nothing there ever happens suddenly. Everything in a school cafeteria happens after waiting in a slooooooooowwwwwww line that doesn't move because some kid at the front of the line can't decide between the corn dog or the salad. To be fair, it is not an easy choice. One is a confusing, crunchy brown lunch item with a strange smell and a low nutritional value. And the other is a corn dog. But that is not important now. What is important is that suddenly . . .

Joules and Kevin looked up from the lunch line into the face of a tall woman with square glasses, a dark purple shirt, and a very large schnoz.

"What do you want?" she asked in a menacing tone, pointing to the large crock of chili.

"Uh . . . ," said Joules.

"Uh . . . ," said Kevin.

"Good choice," said the woman with a sneer.

She slopped a scoop of chili into a small bowl and plopped it onto Kevin's tray. She did the same for Joules and turned to the next kid in line. Her nose bobbled up and down as she shifted impatiently from foot to foot.

"What do you want?"

Joules and Kevin ran to their table and set down their trays.

"She's the one I saw in the hallway right before Mr. H disappeared," said Joules, "and in the woods yesterday. I'm sure of it!"

"You know what this means," said Kevin. "You said that Grunt and Belcher looked like the principal and Mr. Shhh. That means the weird Lunch Lady is the third alien. But whose form is she projecting?"

"It means something else, too," said Joules. "Maybe Mr. H is still alive."

"She might lead us to him," said Kevin as the loudspeaker crackled loudly and a recording blasted through the lunchroom.

"THIS IS AN ANNOUNCEMENT. SCHOOL IS CLOSED. GO HOME, EARTH STUDENTS. COME BACK AT FIVE O'CLOCK WITH YOUR HUMANS AND ALL YOUR SNOTTIE'S TISSUES. SCHOOL IS CLOSED. GO HOME, EARTH STUDENTS. COME BACK AT FIVE O'CLOCK WITH YOUR HUMANS AND ALL YOUR SNOTTIE'S TISSUES. SCHOOL IS . . ."

"School's out! Woo-hoo!"

The students jumped out of their seats, blocking the twins' view of the strange Lunch Lady. Joules climbed onto the bench and scanned the chaotic lunchroom.

"There!" said Kevin, pointing toward the lunchroom door as the woman in purple stepped into a sea of students fleeing the school, and was gone.

Chapter 31

Kevin pulled his notebook from his backpack and plopped it open on the kitchen table.

"We need a plan," he said.

"We need a stick," said Joules, pulling a mop from the closet and a large pair of scissors from a kitchen drawer.

She snipped the long mop strands, which fell to the floor in a pile of fuzzy gray worms.

"That's not a plan," said Kevin.

"Got something better?" asked Joules, propping the bald mop against the wall and reaching for a broom.

Kevin frowned.

"We can do this," he said. "What do we need? What? What? What?"

Kevin impatiently tapped his chart with the end of his pen.

"We know they get energy from stinky things," said Joules. "That stuff they were cooking was smellier than Mom's breakfast. And that's saying something."

"You said they were cooking vats of it," said Kevin.

"Yeah," said Joules.

"Maybe that machine amplifies the smell," said Kevin. "They get energy from smell. That's why they have those big noses. You saw how fast they grew in those cages. They were right by that jala-sauer-fu."

"Maybe," said Joules. "But so what?"

"So . . . ," said Kevin. "Maybe the machine uses that nasty goop and turns it into something their noses can use."

"Yeah?" said Joules. "So what if we use it against them? Make them smell something else."

"Something that combats the smell?" asked Kevin. "Like perfume?"

Joules thought about some of the awful perfume she had smelled at different times in her life.

"That could backfire," she said. "We need to keep Mom and Dad out of the school." Joules picked up the phone and dialed.

Rrrrrrring. Rrrrrrrring. Rrrrrrrring.

Kevin opened the refrigerator. A volcano-shaped orange mound of—food?—jiggled on a ceramic serving platter on the middle shelf of the fridge.

Rrrrrrring. Rrrrrrrring. Rrrrrrrring.

Kevin did not need to take the jiggling volcano out of the fridge to confirm that his mom's cell phone was ringing inside it. Cooking with electronics had become a specialty for his parents after they won the International SPAMathon by accidentally cooking a cell phone into their batter. Since then, all kinds of things popped up inside the Rockmans' dishes. Few of them edible. All of them noisy.

"Try Dad's phone," he said.

Joules dialed. The pie next to the bowl of blue breakfast goop buzzed.

"That stinks!" Kevin said, slamming the refrigerator door.

Joules smiled.

"No it doesn't," said Joules.

"Yes it does!" said Kevin. "We have to stop Mom and Dad, and we can't reach them."

"That's not what I mean," said Joules. "I mean it doesn't stink."

"I don't get it," said Kevin.

Joules walked to the fridge and pulled the door open wide.

"What do you smell?" she asked.

"Nothing," said Kevin. "I'm all stuffed up, remember?"

"Doesn't matter," said Joules. "There's nothing to smell."

"Huh?"

"Why doesn't the fridge stink?" asked Joules, taking out the uncovered bowl of fumilicious breakfast soup.

She sniffed, gagged slightly, and threw the bowl of blue goop into the trash.

"Wow!" she said. "That smells like an elephant's armpit. It really, *really* stinks, but the fridge doesn't."

Kevin looked at his sister in awe.

"You are brilliant!" he said.

"I know," said Joules.

She pulled out the jiggling volcano, pie, and a dozen other weird things from the shelf until only a small orange box filled with white powder remained. She pulled the box out of the fridge and tossed a pinch of the gritty white powder into the air.

"Behold our secret weapon!" she said. "Baking soda!"

The white dust tickled Kevin's nose and sent him into a sneezing frenzy.

"Elbow!" said Joules.

Kevin sneezed into his elbow, then wiped his sleeve with a tissue.

"How is that little box of baking soda going to neutralize two vats of nasty alien power-stink?" asked Kevin.

Joules coolly walked into the garage and came back with two five-gallon plastic tubs of baking soda.

"That oughta do it!" she said.

As the son of extreme cooks, Kevin was rarely pleased by the contents of the pantry or the closets or the garage or the van. The possibility of finding something awful was always higher than the possibility of finding something pleasant. At the moment, though, he was delighted.

"This is the beginning of a good plan," said Kevin, flipping pages and writing in his notebook. "We dump baking soda into the pool. It neutralizes their power-stink and shrinks them back to adorable bunny size."

"Exactly!" said Joules.

"Just one problem," said Kevin. "How do we get Grunt and Belcher into the pool?"

"The old-fashioned way," said Joules, reaching for the broom. "We push them."

"It's a good plan," said Kevin. "What could poss—"

Joules gave her brother the stinkiest stink-eye in the history of stink-eyes.

"—uh—good plan."

"Best one we've got," said Joules.

"Only one we've got," said Kevin.

At 4:15, Joules and Kevin Rockman loaded the tubs of baking soda onto a wagon, grabbed the mop and broom, and headed back to TBD School. They followed the same steps they had taken that morning and every morning to school.

They walked silently, because there was nothing to say. Either the baking soda would neutralize the stench that the aliens needed or it would not. If not, there was very little a mop or broom could do to stop the aliens. Still, Joules was happy to have them.

One thing was obvious. If their plan didn't work, the battle that followed would not take a hundred years like the one Shakespeare wrote about in *Henry V*. The war would be over in minutes.

Kevin set back his shoulders, smiled at his sister, and pulled a little harder on the wagon handle.

Once more unto the breach, dear friends, once more.

Chapter 32

The twins dragged the wagon to the door at the back of the gym. They knew it would be unlocked. It had been unlocked since Mr. Shhh "accidentally broke it" with a sledgehammer. Most teachers parked at the front of the building, but Mr. Shhh wanted to spend every possible second in the gym helping the noodle-armed kids of TBD School. He thought that the three minutes it took him to walk from the front entrance to the gym was wasted time. Parking just outside the gym let him get right to work. It also kept his beautiful new convertible from getting crunched by Mr. H, who liked to bird-watch from the driver's seat, which was not a good thing to do while driving in a parking lot.

Joules opened the heavy door and Kevin pulled the wagon into the empty gym. They sneaked to the tiny hall that connected the gym to the aqua center. Quietly, Joules opened the aqua center door and listened.

Silence.

She held the door open and Kevin pulled the wagon

into the enormous bleacher-filled room. Someone had been very busy since the twins had last stepped into the aqua center. Four long tables sat by the main door. Three contained large vats of chili and ladles. The fourth held stacks of enormous plastic bowls and a basket of plastic spoons. A box of ketchup packets sat atop the drum of industrial-strength slaw. Except for the location, it looked like every chili supper at TBD School. In fact, the drum of slaw had been at every supper the kids could remember. Since nobody ate it, Principal Posner saved it for the next year. At the rate it was being eaten, the drum might last forever. It truly was a great investment.

"I don't get it," whispered Joules. "It looks like they really are having the chili supper. Why would they do that?"

"It's a trap," said Kevin. "They'll lure people in with the chili and then make their move. The chili is like—"

"Bait," said Joules.

A shiver ran down Kevin's spine. He imagined his family and his friends and everyone he knew cramming onto the bleachers, waiting for something pleasant to happen. Something that had happened every year since he was little. Something that involved large bowls of delicious chili. Kevin did not know what would happen this time at the TBD School Chili Supper, but he knew it would be anything but pleasant.

"C'mon," he said, pulling the wagon to the tiny pool.

Joules and Kevin unsealed the tubs of baking soda and dumped them, one by one, into the pool. The gritty white powder dissolved into the pool, turning the aquamarine water cloudy for only a moment before it cleared again. A small mound of baking soda landed on the pool deck, but Kevin easily swept it into the pool with the broom. Joules loaded the empty tubs into the wagon and pulled them behind the kayaks.

"Now we wait," said Kevin.

"Now we eat," said Joules.

Chapter 33

Joules ladled out two bowls of chili and handed one to Kevin. They grabbed two plastic spoons and leaned against the wall behind the kayaks. They had not had a good meal all day and hadn't realized how hungry they were until they smelled the delicious chili.

Just as they raised their spoons to eat, the aqua center door flew open and a tall, large-nosed figure in purple stepped through the doorway. It carried a large net like a deep-sea fisherman might use to land a gigantic tuna. Joules and Kevin crouched behind the kayaks and held their breath.

The Lunch Lady walked toward the pool, sniffing the air and looking around warily.

"It's her!" whispered Joules.

The Lunch Lady tilted her head from side to side.

Sniff. Sniff.

She stepped closer to the pool.

Sniff. Sniff.

Closer.

Sniff.

She looked into the water.

Sniff—

Joules and Kevin silently put their bowls on the floor. Joules grabbed the mop and Kevin raised the straw broom above his head like a baseball bat. As he did, a fine cloud of baking soda drifted onto his face and tickled his nose. His eyes watered. He sniffed. Then sniffed again as a sneeze welled up inside him.

Not now, he thought. "Aah . . . aaahhhh . . . aaaahhhhhh—"

Kevin pressed his nose into the crook of his arm and sneezed.

"—choo!"

It was a small sound muffled by his surprisingly absorbent sleeve, but the Lunch Lady whipped around and started toward the kayaks. She took a few steps toward them. Then stopped.

Sniff.

Joules and Kevin froze.

CLUNK.

Somewhere in the school, a door slammed. The Lunch Lady turned her back to the kayaks and tilted her head toward the door. She listened and sniffed the air again.

Sniff. Sniff.

Joules mouthed one word to Kevin: *Now!*

Joules and Kevin burst from behind the rack of kayaks and ran at the large-schnozzled woman, who pivoted toward them. Joules jabbed at her with the mop. The Lunch Lady dodged the mop and swooped her net over Joules's head. With one swift jerk, she pulled Joules to the floor. Kevin swung the broom like a bat.

Swoosh!

The Lunch Lady ducked and the broom missed its mark. She stepped toward Kevin, grabbed the broom mid-handle, and pulled hard, sending Kevin off balance. He hit the glossy floor and skidded onto his back.

"Shhh!" hissed the Lunch Lady. "They're coming!"

Joules wriggled out of the net and grabbed a kayak paddle. She waved it at the Lunch Lady like a lion tamer with a chair.

"We don't have time for this nonsense," said the Lunch Lady. "They're coming."

"Who?" asked Kevin.

"You know who," said the Lunch Lady. "I saw you at their rocket yesterday."

"Who are you?" asked Kevin.

"She's one of them!" said Joules. "She took Mr. H and destroyed the principal and Mr. Shhh."

"Ha!" laughed the Lunch Lady. "Do I look like an alien?"

"Yes!" said Kevin, pulling himself up and grabbing the mop and jabbing it toward her.

The Lunch Lady ripped off her square glasses and stared harshly at the twins.

"Look at my eyes and tell me I'm an alien," she said.

"Don't look, Kevin!" said Joules, turning away.

It was too late. Kevin looked into the eyes of the large-nosed Lunch Lady. Her eyes were big. They were blue. And they were very human.

Chapter 34

Clank!

A door slammed somewhere in the school.

"Hurry!"

The Lunch Lady ran behind the rack of kayaks. Joules and Kevin ran after her and ducked behind the tiny boats just as the aqua center door burst open and two enormous, hairy, and very alien rabbits tumbled into the room, smacking and whapping each other's noses.

Smack! Whap! BAM!

Joules sniffed the air.

"Ugh," she said. "They smell horrible."

The Lunch Lady reached into her pocket and pulled out three pairs of nose plugs. She slipped a pair on her nose and handed one to Joules and one to Kevin.

"Put these on."

"Why should we trust you?" whispered Joules.

A new wave of putrid air wafted by.

The Lunch Lady shot Joules an is-that-a-good-enough-reason kind of look. Joules was impressed. Not everyone could pull off a look like that. She clamped her pair of plugs over her nostrils and nodded to the Lunch Lady.

The Lunch Lady raised her finger to her lips to signal silence.

Kevin started to put his plugs on, but even touching his nose triggered an overwhelming urge to sneeze. He closed his eyes and tried to fight it. He thought about not sneezing. At last, the urge passed, and he stuck the plugs into his pocket.

"They'll make me sneeze," he whispered, pointing to his stuffed-up nose.

156

Crash! *Growl!* **Smack!** Whap! ***BAM!***

The aliens banged against the bleachers and flopped onto the glossy floor. They stood up and rubbed their noses.

"I'm hungry," said Grunt. "Where is that stinky boy you followed from our landing site? He smelled delicious."

Kevin gulped.

"Not now!" said Belcher. "When our brain waves reach maximum capacity, the change will be complete. Then we will control all the humans' brains. They will bring us tissues and all the smelly things. And we can snack on as many humans as we want!"

"Nothing will stop us!"

"Not even butterfly toots!"

Snicker.

Smack!

Giggle.

Whap!

Snort.

BAM!

"You said 'butterfly toots'! Ha! Ha! Ha! Ha!"

Belcher wheezed, grabbed his belly, stamped his puny feet, fell over, and rolled to the edge of the pool.

"Get up!" said Grunt. "I smell humans. We begin."

"Butterfly toots," said Belcher, wiping a tear from the corner of his eye and fighting back a snicker.

Smack!

"Thank you."

"You are welcome."

A moment later, the doors opened and a happy, noisy crowd of tissue-box-carrying parents and students lined up to enter the aqua center. Mr. and Mrs. Rockman stood in line halfway down the hall, chatting happily with Mack's father and the mother of a third grader. Kevin's heart sank. There was no way to stop his parents from coming in. No way to warn them without revealing themselves and losing any chance to stop the aliens.

Joules looked at the happy crowd oblivious to the aliens standing just feet away.

"Why don't they run away?" asked Joules.

"Why would they?" whispered the Lunch Lady. "They see the principal and gym teacher offering them chili." The Lunch Lady added, "My father observed these creatures on their home planet via camera transmissions from the rocket. He called them Foofs and noticed that they could control other creatures with their noses—or, more accurately, with their sense of smell. It was a kind of mind control. My father called it 'smellepathy.'"

Joules shot Kevin a glance. They had read about the E.A.R.S. space program, which sent rockets to distant planets in search of intelligent life in the universe. At camp, they had encountered another set of aliens who had come to Earth because of that program.

"Your father brought them here?"

"He built the rockets and included a homing device in them," she said. "But he didn't realize the dangers. He—"

She stopped.

"Look," she whispered.

Grunt moved to the doorway and blocked the entrance so only a single person could pass at a time. One by one, the chatty people in the hall entered and tossed their boxes of tissues onto the pile. "Good evening, Principal Pos—"

"Silence!" said Grunt. "Eat."

She stared into their faces with her large swirling blue eyes. One by one, the humans fell silent, then walked blankly to Belcher, who handed them a big bowl of chili and a spoon.

"Eat," he said.

"Eat. Eat. Eat," repeated the humans.

They climbed the bleachers, sat down, and began to eat.

Within minutes, the bleachers of the TBD School aqua center were filled with hundreds of people slowly slurping chili, as the two aliens watched with satisfaction.

And smiled.

Chapter 35

"What's going on?" asked Kevin.

"They're waiting," said the Lunch Lady. "The aliens' brains and noses are intricately connected. As their noses are activated by smells, their brains get hot. When that happens, their smellepathy will grow. If their brains get hot enough, their smellepathy will reach a state of hyperpower and become permanent."

"Then what?" asked Kevin.

"Then we are in big trouble," said Joules. "Big stink + big schnoz + extreme metabolism = brain-fusing power that will take over the world."

"They'll be unstoppable!" said Kevin.

"We'll stop them," said Joules.

She looked at her parents blankly slurping chili on the bleachers in the sea of zombified humans.

"We have to."

"We have to vaporize the pool water and neutralize the smell," said Kevin.

The Lunch Lady looked impressed.

"Interesting idea," she said. "How would you do that?"

"The Foofs built a machine," said Kevin. "We think that's what it does. At least we hope so."

"Where is it?"

Her question was quickly answered. Belcher left the aqua center and returned a moment later, dragging the giant contraption with a new set of Noodle-Armor. Clearly, Mr. Shhh's invention was good for one thing: It made a great harness to pull enormous contraptions!

A third alien rabbit walked behind the contraption, carrying a large vat of goop that splished and sploshed onto the floor in green puddles. Joules and Kevin tried to see the alien's face, but the vat blocked their view.

Belcher positioned the contraption a few inches from the pool and dropped the end of its nozzle into the water. He flipped the switch and clapped his enormous hands gleefully. The machine sputtered and shuddered. A high-pitched whine rose above the slurping noise of the crowd.

The third alien carried the vat of goop to the pool and dumped it into the water. Instantly, the water turned from aqua blue to nasty brown. The alien put down the vat and, for the first time, the twins looked at his face, carefully avoiding eye contact. The enormous greasy gray rabbit wore a pair of round glasses and a tweed hat.

Joules and Kevin gasped. It was Mr. H—or a projection of him, anyway. Anger rose up inside Joules. She burst out from behind the kayaks, her eyes stinging as she blinked back tears.

"Mr. H!"

Kevin ran after his sister, who was charging "Mr. H" with the mop handle.

"Joules!" yelled Kevin.

The Lunch Lady raced past Kevin and reached the pool just as Joules slammed the mop handle into "Mr. H's" chest. His round glasses and tweed hat flew off his head and he stumbled backward, arms flailing desperately in the air. As he tumbled into the pool, he grabbed Joules's arm and the Lunch Lady's ankle. He splashed into the deep brown water, dragging Joules and the Lunch Lady with him.

Down, down, down they plummeted into the dark water. Joules let go of the mop handle and kicked hard against the enormous sinking alien. The alien tightened his grip on her wrist and she kicked again. Her foot landed hard and she did it again. The alien let go and she pushed toward the surface of the tiny pool. Kevin grabbed her hand and helped her from the water. She stood on the deck, coughing up nasty brown fluid.

A moment later, the Lunch Lady popped to the surface of the pool, splashing frantically. Kevin pulled her to the deck beside Joules.

A heartbeat later, the Foof burst smoothly out of the brown water and flopped like a seal upon the deck. He stood and shook like a dog, spraying greasy brown water throughout the aqua center.

Suddenly, Joules and the Lunch Lady stopped coughing, stood upright, and stared blankly into the air. Joules turned to the wet alien and smiled vacantly.

"Hello, Mr. H," she said. "I am glad you are alive."

Kevin grabbed his sister's arm, but she pulled free and stepped closer to the soggy alien. Without looking, she pushed Kevin in the chest, knocking him to the deck.

Joules leaned close to the six-foot-tall soggy rabbit, pressed her head against its rough gray fur, and gave him a hug.

At that moment, two neon-pink pairs of nose plugs popped to the surface of the slimy brown water, floated for a moment, and then sank slowly out of sight.

Chapter 36

"Joules!" yelled Kevin. "Pinch your nose!"

It was too late. Joules's eyes swirled wildly.

"Snap out of it, Joules!"

"Eat," she said.

Kevin got up and shook the Lunch Lady's shoulder.

"Wake up!" he yelled.

"Eat," she said.

"Ha ha ha!" said Grunt. "We control them!"

"The smelly boy is here," said Belcher. "It is snack time!"

Belcher pushed close to Kevin, eyes swirling and schnoz bobbing up and down.

Kevin turned away and squeezed his eyes shut.

"He is not very stinky," said Grunt. "What is wrong with him?"

Belcher poked Kevin in the chest with his claw.

"He needs sauce," said the third alien, shaking like a dog and spraying Kevin with brown pool water.

"Let us eat him now!" said Belcher. "I want a snack."

"Not yet!" said Grunt. "Our power is not complete. We finish the process. Then we have snacks!"

"I like snacks," said the third alien. "The science man was not a good snack."

"His name was Mr. H!" yelled Kevin. "You destroyed him!"

"That is a silly name," said the alien. "Commander Lulupovichatoot is a better name."

Snicker.

"You said 'toot,'" said Belcher.

Smack!

Giggle.

Whap!

Chuckle. Wheeze.

Whap!

Silence.

"Thank you, Commander Lulu," said Belcher. "I needed that."

Commander Lulu turned back to the contraption and twisted a large dial. The machine sputtered faster, and a clear tube sucked brown liquid into the boiler. The machine coughed. Puffs of white smoke shot out of a vent and drifted over the aliens. They sniffed the smoke hungrily and thumped their tiny feet rapidly on the pool deck.

Commander Lulu cranked the dial again and the smoke belched, brown and thick, into the air. The Foofs inhaled deeply as the nozzle slurped water from the pool and vaporized it. Kevin waited for the vaporized baking soda to neutralize the stench.

That's it, Kevin thought. *Big, big breaths. Breathe it in!*

The aliens breathed deeper and deeper still. But as he watched, they fluffed their fur and showed their fangs. Their eyes swirled faster. The goop was too strong. The aliens stared at the crowd and concentrated. The humans stopped slurping their chili and stared straight at the swirly eyes of the Foofs, whose powers were growing stronger by the moment.

The humans began to chant.

"We obey. We obey."

"Joules!" yelled Kevin. "Snap out of it!"

"Obey. Obey. Obey."

The Foofs' schnozzles bounced wildly and they drummed their feet faster and faster. They stretched taller and taller. Kevin watched as the enormous rabbits loomed over his sister and the Lunch Lady.

The crowd chanted louder and louder.

"Obey! Obey! Obey!"

"It's working!" said Grunt. "But we need more power! More!"

Commander Lulu rolled the industrial drum of slaw to the edge of the pool, pried off the lid, and smelled the soupy concoction of cabbage and clear liquid.

He pulled back from the industrial drum and bared his fangs.

"This will do it!" said Commander Lulu.

Kevin looked at the industrial vat of slaw and then at his parents chanting from the bleachers. He had helped his mom make slaw a hundred times. Would he ever get to help her grate the cabbage, and pour the vinegar over . . . *Uh-oh*, thought Kevin . . . *Oh no* . . .

Kevin looked at the giant vat of vinegar-drenched cabbage and at the brown pool water. Water that contained a very, *very* large amount of the one thing you never want to mix with vinegar.

Baking soda.

Kevin watched in horror as Commander Lulu tipped the vat and poured a river of vinegar into the brown pool.

What have we done? he thought. *What have we done?*

Chapter 37

FWOOOOOSH!!!!!

The pool erupted like a twenty-megaton science fair volcano.

A foamy brown tidal wave roared over the Foofs, the twins, and the Lunch Lady. It slammed into the crowded bleachers.

Then, as fast as it had begun, it was gone. Only the sound of popping foam bubbles and the slurping of chili remained.

The small, deep pool was now almost empty, but outside the pool, everything and everybody was drenched with brown liquid and covered with limp strands of brownish cabbage. Pools of foamy slaw dotted the aqua center floor, and a brown mist lingered in the air.

The contraption sputtered twice, spewed a wad of cabbage into the air, and died. At least the explosion had wiped out the machine. But was it in time? Kevin looked hopefully at the Foofs, but as he watched, they breathed the damp mist that filled the aqua center air and laughed.

"Ha!" said Grunt. "My brain is hot."

"Mine is hot!"

"Hot!"

They stepped closer to Kevin, their noses wobbling.

Sniff! Sniff!

Suddenly, Kevin's vision blurred and his head throbbed. He tried to squeeze his eyes shut as a sharp pain stabbed the inside of his nose, but he could not even blink.

"Ha! Smelly Boy!" laughed Commander Lulu. "You lose! The change is done! Now we shall control you, too!"

As Kevin looked at the aliens, Belcher suddenly grew blurry. His long, floppy ears folded flat and morphed into human hair. His fur blurred into a sweat suit and sneakers. For a moment, the rabbit took on Mr. Shhh's form. Mr. H and Principal Posner stood next to him.

Their smellepathy was now strong enough to penetrate Kevin's brain even through his clogged nose. He felt weak. His arms seemed to weigh a thousand pounds. Slowly, he raised his arms and pinched his nostrils closed. Immediately, the aliens blurred slightly and became half-alien once more.

"Ha!" laughed Belcher. "We are not done!"

But after only a moment, Kevin's vision blurred and the aliens again appeared in the form of the teachers they had destroyed. Kevin tried to look away or close his eyes, but he could not. The aliens' voices spoke directly to his brain. Their voices drummed inside his head.

"Obey! Obey! Obey!"

The crowd chanted.

"Obey! Obey! Obey!"

"Ha ha!" said Belcher. "Let's eat!"

They stepped toward Kevin, licked their lips, and drummed their feet frantically.

The humans in the bleachers chanted louder and louder.

"Eat! Eat! Eat!"

When suddenly . . . the aqua center air-conditioning kicked in and an icy breeze blasted down from the ceiling, blowing away the damp mist. Kevin shook his head as the teachers blurred into aliens once more. Their voices faded from Kevin's brain. The change was *not* complete. There was hope.

Commander Lulu slammed the machine with a great furry fist. "More!"

WHACK!

"We need more!" said Grunt, inhaling deeply.

"More!" yelled Belcher, kicking the machine. The

contraption tumbled into the pool and broke into pieces in the shallow brown water.

Splash!

The Foofs growled and shrank.

"Ha!" yelled Kevin. "It didn't work!"

"Ha ha!" laughed Grunt. "You are a silly person, Smelly Boy! You do not know anything! The brown water made us strong. They will do the rest!"

"Who?" asked Kevin. "Who will do the rest? What are you talking about?"

The answer was clear.

The Foofs pointed at the humans in the bleachers.

"They will!"

The humans stood up suddenly, raised their bowls to their lips, and slurped the last of their chili. As they did, a wave of terror rushed over Kevin as he remembered the pile of cans in the kitchen.

Cans of chili sauce.

Cans of tomatoes.

And cans of beans.

So very, *very* many beans.

Toot.

Kevin listened in horror as the sound erupted quietly

near the back of the bleachers. He looked at the enormous bean-eating crowd and gasped.

Toot.

Another one flew from the second row.

TOOT!

From somewhere at the right.

TOOT! TOOT!

TOOT! TOOT! TOOT!

Snicker.

TOOT!

"Hee hee," said Belcher. "They tooted."

SMACK!

TOOT!

As the sound (and smell) of tooting filled the aqua center, the aliens began once more to grow. Their shapes blurred.

Kevin watched as the aliens grew. He watched as the change accelerated. At any moment, it would be complete.

TOOT!

Snicker.

"Hee hee!"

"Ha ha ha! You are stinky!"

Belcher tilted to one side.

"Ha! Ha! Ha!" he laughed.

He fell backward and kicked his tiny feet in the air.

He kicked Joules square in the nose. She doubled over and pinched her thumbs over her nostrils as a trail of red liquid trickled down her face.

As if a spell had been broken, Joules shook her head and looked around. Her head swam and she felt faint. She tried to run, but her feet were frozen in place. She could not speak. The brain waves of the Foofs reached her mind once more, and she felt her willpower slipping away.

She looked at Kevin, who stood with his hand a few inches from his nose. His eyes watered and his face twitched weirdly. At that moment, Joules knew exactly how to stop the aliens, whose extreme metabolism had now kicked into high gear. They grew faster and faster as Kevin fought the sneeze.

"Aaaah—

"Aaaaaaaah—"

Joules struggled to speak, but only a muffled "MMMMMM" sound came out. It was quickly drowned by the sound of tooting humans and snickering aliens.

"MMMMMM!" she tried again.

Kevin looked at her through watering eyes.

Joules shot a look at Kevin's elbow, then at the aliens. She did it again.

AAAAAAAAAAAHHHHHHHH—

Kevin raised his elbow halfway to his nose, then stopped. He looked at Joules. He smiled. He lowered his elbow and . . .

AAAAAAAAAAAAAHHHHHH-CHOOOOOOOOO!

Kevin sneezed the greatest sneeze in the history of all sneezes. Millions of microscopic droplets sprayed out of his nose at a rate of 100 miles per hour, coating the three laughing Foofs with a glistening mist. The laughing Foofs breathed in the mist.

They coughed.

They sneezed.

Kevin's germs latched onto the Foofs' extreme metabolism with extreme force. In moments, their schnozzles were completely blocked with enormous green globs of mucus as thick as clay. They could not smell. They could not absorb the delicious putrid stench of the aqua center air and transform the smells into dangerous superpowers. And so, they shrank.

And shrank.

And shrank.

Chapter 38

As the Foofs shrank, so did their control over the humans. The crowd awakened from the trance that had gripped them since the moment they had stepped into the aqua center. One by one, they looked around in confusion, took a breath, and smelled something not at all pleasant, if you know what we mean, and we're pretty sure you do if you've ever eaten too much chili or lived with anyone who has.

They glanced around awkwardly, innocently whistled a little song, and walked quickly away.

Within moments, the crowd was gone. Only the twins and the Lunch Lady remained.

"Brilliant action!" she said. "How clever to utilize their extreme metabolism against them! I shudder to think what might have happened had we not stopped these horrible, vile creatures."

She grabbed the fishing net and scooped up the tiny bunnies, who sat blinking on the pool deck.

"Who are you?" asked Joules.

"My name is Lil," she said. "Lil Dewdy."

Snicker.

The Lunch Lady glared at Joules.

"I am the daughter of Professor Donald J. Dewdy," she said.

Snicker.

"How original," said the Lunch Lady. "If you are quite finished . . . I am looking for my father, Professor Donald J. Dewdy."

"Sorry," said Kevin.

"We read about him at the NASA facility," Joules said. "What happened to him?"

"I wish I knew," said Miss Lil. "He disappeared a year ago. He recorded his findings in a book, which he showed me once. Perhaps if I could find the book, it might give me some clue about what happened to him."

Miss Lil straightened her square glasses and cleared her throat.

"In any case," she said, "my father's rockets brought these aliens to Earth, and I feel responsible for them. I tracked them to this school. I had to stop them, so I went undercover and became a lunch lady. I'm just glad that you kids were here to help. But now we must do something with these creatures."

"I think they should go to Miss Bee's kindergarten class," said Joules.

"Of course," said Miss Lil softly. "Kindergarten is a fine environment for rabbits. Especially ones who gain energy from unpleasant odors. I'm sure they would be very happy in Miss Bee's room. What could possibly be smelly in a kindergarten classroom?"

Joules and Kevin looked at each other.

"Enjoy your rabbits," said Kevin.

"Yep," said Joules. "They're all yours."

Miss Lil smiled.

"I shall keep them far from dangerous odors, I assure you."

She hoisted the net of wriggling, big-schnozzled bunnies over her shoulder and walked away.

Chapter 39

Joules and Kevin found their parents in the school parking lot, chatting with a woman with red hair. They did not recognize her.

"Who is—"

BAM!

A red-shoed mummy slammed into Joules, nearly knocking her over.

"Watch out!" yelled Kevin.

"Mmmmmm," said the mummy.

Joules yanked a loose bandage on the mummy's waist, sending the mummy twirling across the parking lot. In just a moment, the bandages lay in a heap on his red high-top sneakers.

"Nelson?"

Indeed, it was.

Those of you brave enough to have read *Attack of the Fluffy Bunnies* will remember that Nelson was a friend from Camp Whatsitooya. Nelson's knowledge of plumbing helped save the day when a very bad situation arose involving alien rabbits. You will also remember that Nelson was the boy who never stopped talking. Ever.

"Hi," said Nelson, who was swaying like a seasick sailor. "It's me! Aren't you glad to see me? I've been trying to talk to you for months. Ever since we moved here. We moved here after I told Mom all about you guys. She thought you sounded nice and the town sounded nice so we just moved. Isn't that nice? I think that's nice. Mom says I need more friends so that I'll quit watching so much TV and get out more. I guess she's right. Do you think she's right? I think she's right. But I don't know. I've

While Nelson told the twins about everything (and we mean absolutely every little thing) that had happened to him since camp ended, Nelson's mother told Mr. and Mrs. Rockman all about the wonderful impression camp had made on Nelson and how she was planning to send him back this summer. The camp had been bought by someone new. An acting troupe, which had turned it into a theater camp.

Had Kevin and Joules not been enjoying the fresh, cool night air as they walked down the sidewalk, been here for months, but I kept getting wrapped up by the principal. Mom said she kept wrapping me up because it was the school dress code, so I just started dressing like that on my own. I think that was a good idea. Do you think that was a good idea? I think it was a good idea. Except that the bandages are kind of scratchy . . .

Hey! Did you ever watch that show about plumbing that I liked? Remember, I told you about it? It doesn't matter, because they canceled it. Can you imagine that? I couldn't believe it. But then I found a really great show on the Geography Channel. You would not

their minds being lulled into a dreamy state by Nelson's melodic and endless ramblings, they might have heard their mother say something like "The twins would love to go back to summer camp!"

They might also have heard their father say, "I'm sure it would be a delightful and very educational experience. Perhaps they have brochures. I do love brochures."

They might also have heard their parents say, "What a great idea to have a theater camp in the middle of the woods next to an abandoned NASA rocket facility. It would be a very safe environment. Imagine believe it. It is called *The States*. And guess what it's about? Guess! Yeah! The states. First, they told everything about Alabama. Then they did Alaska. Then they did Arizona, Arkansas, California, Colorado, Con

the fun the kids would have putting on musicals and learning to dance and sing and act. Perhaps they could even explore that abandoned NASA rocket facility. Every kid needs to learn about music and science. There might even be marshmallows. And after all, what could possibly go wrong?"

What indeed?

Oh yes . . .

Famous Last Words.

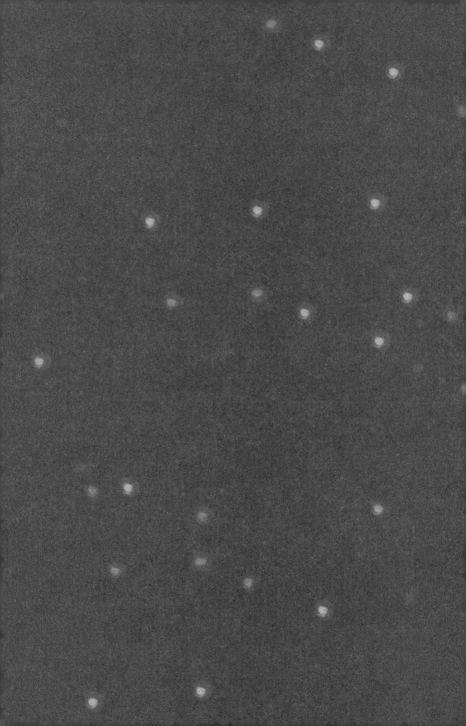